T0095136

COLD FROM THE INSIDE OUT

One Woman's Escape to Adventure and a New Life

Violeta F. Sterner

Order this book online at www.trafford.com
or email orders@trafford.com

Most Trafford titles are also available at major online book retailers.

This is a work of fiction. All of the characters, names, incidents, organizations,
and dialogue in this novel are either the products of the author's imagination
or are used fictitiously.

Printed in the United States of America.

ISBN: 978-1-4269-3932-7 (sc)
ISBN: 978-1-4269-3933-4 (hc)
ISBN: 978-1-4269-3970-9 (e)

Library of Congress Control Number: 2010910594

Trafford rev. 01/03/2011

 www.trafford.com

North America & international
toll-free: 1 888 232 4444 (USA & Canada)
fax: 812 355 4082

SHE WAS LOST LONG before the snow began to fall. She knew she made a wrong turn, but believed it was correctable. It was such a beautiful drive. Winding through the mountains, she crossed no other roads, there were no houses, no people, and she met no other vehicles. There was no cell phone reception. There was no help. She was not alarmed until the snow became serious. It grew heavier as she continued driving. Soon it covered the trees, the bushes, the road, and her car. It was a world of white. Now she was not only lost, she was lost and afraid. She was alone on a mountain road to nowhere in a BLIZZARD!

Stop this, her brain ordered! Panic will not help you. Maybe you should stop. Stop where and for why? There was no help on this road, no one to turn to. Just freeze to death calmly. Don't make a fuss. They say it's just like going to sleep. They say it does not hurt. What do they know? They are not the ones in danger of freezing to death.

What is that up ahead?

Flashing lights – flashing red lights. Maybe there were people. She would be much calmer if there were people. Closer, it was closer now. It was – a school bus – in the middle of the road – in the middle of nowhere – all its flashers going like it was stopping for kids. Maybe it wasn't in the middle of nowhere. It was a school bus stopping for children. Where were the children? Why didn't she see any children? Were they already gone inside? There were no buildings, where were the children? Were the children on the bus? The windows were frosted and snow was collecting in the corners. Was that movement inside the bus? Were there children on the bus?

Driving on was not an option. She rolled to a stop slowly, not too close to the back of the bus. Leaving the car running, she made her way to the door of the bus and knocked - sort of. The door flew open and there she saw a boy. He was a beautiful child and showed no sigh of fear or even surprise.

1

"Hi, my name is Lucas," he greeted her, "and this is my brother, Tristan."

Another child joined the first and she would have thought she was seeing double except for the eyes. Lucas' were black, shining and dark. Tristan's were green, a glowing green that reminded her of forests and jungles and places that man had not touched.

"Hello, my name is Kate," she responded. "Is everyone OK in here? Where is your driver? How long have you been stranded here?" She rapid fired the questions.

The boys answered them in order. "Yes, we are OK. The driver went for help when the bus died. We don't know how long it's been, but long enough to run out of gas and lose all the heat in the bus."

Kate nodded her head, thinking quickly. She knew they had to leave.

"Do you know where this road goes?" she asked Lucas.

"Sure," he replied. "It leads down to HWY 21, which will take us to the High Valley"

"Is it far to the Valley? Can we make it by nightfall?"

"Don't you know where you are?" asked Tristan.

"No" replied Kate. "I've been lost for several hours, but since I have a car, and you know how to get out of here, I suggest we all go together."

Luc and Trist, for that is already how she thought of them, looked at the other children, who simply nodded to indicate they were ready to go.

"All right, let's see if we can get everyone in the seats without unloading the back. Luc and Trist, I'll need you in the front to give directions," said Kate as she started down the steps.

All the children piled into the car without comment. She counted nine. She had no idea her small SUV would hold that many people, but she was glad everyone fit without hassle or argument.

I could really use a cigarette, she thought as she climbed into the driver's seat. Not now, responded the alternate side of her brain. It's no time to be distracted while driving. Therefore, she eased around the bus and continued slowly down the road. The children were all quiet, grateful for the heat, except for Luc and Trist, who did running commentary on where they were and what was to come. It bounced effortlessly between them as they finished each other's sentences and continued each other's thoughts.

They were on a slight downward slope around a big looping curve when she saw a strange lump in the middle of the road. She thought it must be road kill until Bobby sang out with, "That's John Paul!"

"What is a John Paul?" Kate asked.

"Our bus driver," they all replied in unison.

Kate carefully brought the car to a stop, but again did not cut the engine.

John Paul lay face down, covered with snow. He had been here for some time. Kate searched for and found a pulse. It was slow and weak, but it was there. Luc dribbled a little snow into his mouth and he swallowed as it melted.

They needed to get John Paul into the car. They knew he would be no help to them. Despite their best efforts, he remained unconscious.

Kate repositioned the car to put the front passenger door close to John Paul. With Kate and most of the children working together, they managed to get John Paul levered into the car, at least most of him was in the car. The road was slick. There was ice under the snow. Kate just needed to finish tucking John Paul up a bit and they were on their way.

As Kate attempted to get both his legs folded into, what now appeared to be her small front seat floorboard, John Paul stiffened and spasm after spasm ripped through him. One of his wild swings caught Kate, throwing her to the ground where she landed hard on her left side. She had been so careful, tried so hard not to slip, and then she was falling. The cold bare highway kissed her hip and the side of her head violently. The children all heard her land and feared that something was broken, leaving them stranded again.

Kate moaned and they crowded round her. They knew she needed help, but seemed paralyzed to do anything. When they began to ask questions, they all came at her in a jumble.

Kate was still conscious, which was good. She was in great pain, which was bad. Luc finally took charge of the little group. He was neither the largest nor the oldest, but he was the most stubborn.

They packed snow against her left side, especially her head, to try to manage the swelling. Kate soon began to complain about the cold. Both Luc and Trist considered that a good sign.

"Kate, we know its cold, but it needs to be done. Now we need to know if anything is broken," said Trist.

Kate replied distinctly, "My head is broken." The boys did not know exactly what she meant, but at least she was coherent and responsive. They proceeded to check her for broken bones. The hip and leg did not appear to be broken. She could move them, albeit with great difficulty and pain. Her left arm had somehow escaped the worst of the impact and was moving easily, if not quickly.

"Can any of you drive?" Kate suddenly asked. All the children looked uneasy. Most had bragged at one time or another of their adventures behind the wheel, but none really had any experience and now they had to admit it.

"I can't hear you! Can anybody drive? We are stuck here." Kate prompted a response.

Melissa finally answered, "No ma'am. No one can drive."

"Kate, Kate! Don't go to sleep. That's bad. We could all freeze here. You can't go to sleep"

It came at her loud and quick from all sides while several hands shook her urgently to get her attention.

"Okay, Okay" she sluggishly focused on the faces staring down at her. How creepy. Looked like a funeral with her as the corpse. She needed to move now. Way too creepy.

"Help me up!" Abrupt and clear, this startled several of the children and made them jump.

"That's not really a good idea, Kate. How are you going to drive? You certainly can't walk, and you need rest and… ", Luc argued, but Kate interrupted. "Make up your mind: no walking, no driving, and no flying. Well, we need to get out of here. Driving seems best. I'm too tired for walking. It's too cold, and too slick, very slick for walking." She wasn't really rambling, but she wasn't exactly making sense either. This could be ugly and all the children knew it. Who were they kidding? It was already ugly.

"Help me up!" she said, and they did. Gently and slowly, they got her upright, around the car and into the driver's seat. They tucked in John Paul and everyone else jammed into the back seat, with Luc balanced between the front seats so he could give direction and grab the wheel if needed

Slowly, so very slowly, they moved through the white world. They managed to stay on paved roads – mostly, and not be stuck anywhere. In their efforts to keep Kate awake, they sang songs, took turns telling jokes, and reciting anything they had memorized, but their memories soon ran dry and the car became quiet, but it kept moving. Slowly, erratically, but always moving, they made their way toward – who knew where, but it had heat and food, and a place to sleep. She really needed to sleep.

They were climbing higher in the mountains. "Luc, aren't we going up? Why are we going up?" she asked finally.

"Yes ma'am" he responded promptly. "We have to go a little higher to get to the High Valley."

"What is a High Valley?" Kate asked.

"That's home," came promptly from both Luc and Trist.

"How high is it?" asked Kate

"About 9000 feet," they responded.

"Then why is it called the High Valley?"

"Cause it's the last one on the way up the mountains."

"Can't we go someplace closer?" asked Kate

"It's the closest safe place to where we are," replied Trist. "We'll be there soon if we keep moving."

They kept moving, until Luc finally pointed to what he said was a road and told her it was the last one home.

"That goes into the side of a mountain. Even through the snow, I can see that," said Kate.

"No, it doesn't. There's a gate," said Luc.

"A gate, there's a gate in the mountain?"

"More like a tunnel," said Trist. We just call it the gate because it's easier.

"A tunnel, when we get through the tunnel we'll be in the High Valley?"

"Right," said both boys.

"Just like Alice down the rabbit hole," said Kate.

"Who's Alice?" asked Bobby, looking around the car. Nobody knew, everybody shrugged, and Kate began to laugh desperately.

Through the tunnel they went, and emerged into the valley, or she assumed they were in the valley. It was snowing faster. It was blowing harder. They could have been anywhere.

"Just stay on the road until you reach the house," said Luc. "We're close now. Just a little longer and we'll be home."

"Is this the house?" asked Kate, as the shadow of a building appeared off to her right.

"No, that's one of the barns," said Trist. "We'll pass another one, a bigger one, before we get to the house."

"What do you keep in these big barns?" asked Kate?

"Horses." said Luc.

"We breed horses." from Trist.

"They have really pretty horses," from two of the smaller children.

"There's somebody out there. Look, somebody's moving," said Trist.

"Is this the house," asked Kate?

"No, it's further on, but there are people here. They can help," said Luc.

"We need to keep moving until we stop," said Kate.

"That makes no sense," said Luc. "We can stop here."

"Let her go" said Trist. "She's too tired and too hurt to think."

As they passed the barn, they saw snowmobiles pulled up next to the road and shadowy figures moving around them. The movement stopped as they went past and the children put down the car windows and waved to get attention.

Soon the second barn passed, and still the car kept moving. Slowly and steadily, no sudden stops, no sudden accelerations, no sudden turns, the car finally came to a gentle stop by the front porch.

As the children piled joyously out of the car, talking and laughing, Kate sat watching the windshield wipers work and the snow continue to accumulate.

The snowmobiles returned to the house. Inside it was warm and dry clothes appeared as wet ones were removed. Luc and Trist explained to their father how John Paul was hurt, how Kate found them in the school bus and was hurt saving John Paul, and how she had brought them safely to the valley.

"Where is she?" Da asked. To the rest of the world he was Ravenwood, but to his children, he was Da.

"Where is she?" he asked again. The children realized she was not with them in the house, which meant she probably never left the car.

"She hurt her head badly and she was really worn out when we got here," said Trist.

Da simply nodded and went out to check the car. They watched as he opened the driver's side door, reached in, and turned off the ignition.

"She's still in the car. Why did she stay in the car," Luc whispered. It seemed very spooky that she was still in the car, like maybe something more had happened to her and they just didn't know it yet.

Then Da knelt down to her level and began to talk, so they knew she was still alive. After a few minutes, he reached out and turned her face to him to get her attention. She had remained staring at the snow through the windshield and only now focused on his face.

"Hello Kate. My name is Ravenwood. Do you know who I am?" asked Ravenwood.

"You're the father of Luc and Trist," she replied.

"That's right. You're all safe now. The house is warm and there is room for everyone. Let's go inside."

She tried to move her leg out the open car door, but nothing happened and she just stared at it as if it didn't belong to her.

"Luc told me how you were hurt and Trist says you're exhausted. Let's get you inside." He placed her arms around his neck and lifted her easily from the car.

"Oh. I'm too heavy," she said, to which he chuckled and continued up the front porch steps and into the house.

The warmth surrounded her as soon as they passed through the front door; so warm and her head began to droop.

"No sleeping Kate. You've had a head injury. Mr. Po needs to look at you. No sleeping for now," stressed Ravenwood.

"What's a Mr. Po?" asked Kate.

"We've already been through that," said Trist. "I think she just likes the sound of the question."

Ravenwood sat her in a large chair in the main room and began removing her wet shoes, while Trist brought a towel for her hair. The children spread across the floor in various positions and states or dress. They were comfortable, warm, and munching on something from a large bowl by the hearth. As Kate began to drift again, she felt someone take her hand, someone small.

"Mama, you have to stay awake. Da said so." Kate looked to her left and saw a lovely girl about three years old. She had large green eyes and skin so fair all the veins in the side of her face showed blue through the skin. Her hair was red, not a frizzy bright red, but more like embers in a dying fire red.

"Hello, little woman," said Kate. "What's your name?"

"Brynna," replied the child.

"I like it. It is so soft, flowing, and beautiful. My name is Kate."

"Da says you have to stay awake," said Brynna.

"Ravenwood is your father," inquired Kate?

"Yes. Luc and Trist and Sela and Gabe and me," said the child.

"There are 5 of you? That's a nice crowd," said Kate.

Ravenwood came to move her to the kitchen and Brynna wanted to go with.

"I want to help take care of Mama," said Brynna stubbornly.

"I know, but right now I need you to help with the other children while Mr. Po looks after Mama," said Ravenwood. "Can you do that for me?"

"Yes Da. You'll make sure she's all right?"

"Yes Bryn. I'll make sure."

Somewhat mollified, she marched over to straighten the blankets over little Lizbet Hayes while Ravenwood moved Kate onto the kitchen island counter. It was a large island and used to treat injuries, among other things.

"Hello, Kate. My name is Mr. Po," said a voice just behind and to the left of Ravenwood.

Looking over, she saw an oriental man of average size, she guessed about 50, but maybe a little older.

"I'm going to start with your hip and then we'll take a look at your head, Ok," asked Mr. Po?

"How is the bus driver?" asked Kate.

"He's still alive, thanks to you and the children," Mr. Po replied. "Looks like some kind of stroke. Once the snow stops, we'll take him to the hospital. Tests should tell us what it was."

"What are you doing?" asked Kate, suspicion, bubbling in her voice. "You can't just start removing my clothes in the middle of the kitchen."

"I can remove them somewhere else later, but right now Mr. Po needs to check your hip," said Ravenwood reasonably.

"But – but we're in the middle of the kitchen", protested Kate.

"So you said," Ravenwood responded. Her shoes and socks were gone and her pants half way off when Mr. Po returned with a blanket.

"Perhaps this will help," Mr. Po, volunteered. "You are in no danger here, but right now your modesty is not our primary consideration." He placed the blanket partially over her lower legs and tucked the corner into her hand, while Ravenwood finished removing the pants.

"Knickers off?" asked Ravenwood.

"Yes"-replied Mr. Po.

Kate tried to protest, but they were already gone. Ravenwood had not bothered with sliding them off, but slit them up the sides and pulled them free. He tucked the blanket higher around her in the same motion.

"We need to turn her onto her right side. The boys said she fell hard on her left," said Mr. Po. Slowly they rolled her onto her right side. She tried not to protest, but little moans and gasps escaped as they moved her.

"I need you to move your leg for me. I will support it and you need to bend it. Very good, now, I'm going to move it. Just relax your muscles and let me make sure it's not broken," said Mr. Po.

Mr. Po moved the leg through a series of positions. When her moans grew louder, Ravenwood gave her his hand and said, "Squeeze as hard as you need to." She clung to the hand as Mr. Po moved her through various positions. With his fingers, he probed and felt his way all along the bone and checked the movement until he was satisfied nothing was broken.

"That is a really severe bruise, but not a break," said Mr. Po.

"Told you my head is broken," responded Kate immediately.

"I'll get to that next, but I'm going to pack some ice around your hip to see if we can slow down that bruise. All the way from your waist to your knee, it's already showing under the skin. It will continue to get worse for several hours at least. We'll do some light massage to try and move the collected blood, but you're going to have a rainbow across that hip for a while." He disappeared briefly, only to return with enough ice to pack her whole body. After placing it around her hip and tucking up her blanket, he said, "Now let's take a look at your head."

Mr. Po began gently to explore the left side of her head. "I will try to be quick. I know it hurts," he told her. Kate just squeezed Ravenwood's hand tighter, but did not say a word. He looked into her eyes, used a flashlight to check for reaction of her pupils, made her follow his finger with her eyes, and a few other basic checks. Then he felt his way across the left side of her head again, taking note of when she winced and how hard she squeezed Ravenwood's hand. She knew he was finished when he packed the ice around her head and told her not to move too much and not to fall asleep.

"When can I sleep," asked Kate quietly?

"Not for a while," replied Mr. Po. "There is the possibility of concussion, so we need to keep you at least semi-conscious for the next 22-24 hours."

"I can't do that. I am so tired. I just need to sleep, just for a little," said Kate.

"Kate, this is very important. Look at me!" said Ravenwood in a voice that demanded attention. His voice was deep and usually low. Sometimes it sounded almost creaky, as though it got very little use. Now he rapped out the words as though giving commands to the latest Marine recruit.

"Kate, you will open your eyes and look at me. Pay attention. It's important that you stay awake. Look at me. Will you try if we help you?" urged Ravenwood.

"You will help me to stay awake?" asked Kate. Her voice was softer and the words had begun to slur, but the question was still clear.

"Yes." assured Ravenwood. "We will help, but you must try. Will you do that?"

"Yes, Jacob. I will try," promised Kate. Ravenwood looked at her intently with a smile flickering across his face.

"Thank you, Kate. I'll see about finding you some clothes."

"Warm. We need warm," urged Kate as he went toward the main room.

Mr. Po took Ravenwood's place on the stool in front of Kate, helping her to focus until Ravenwood came back with some clothing.

"Warm, as ordered" he assured her.

It would be some time before the ice bath ended and they allowed her to dress. Everything worked fine, with a little modification, except the sweatshirt. Kate happily pulled on the next layer of clothing until she got to the final sweatshirt.

"Too small," she said distinctly.

"It's a men's small," replied Ravenwood. "It should fit if we roll up the sleeves."

"Too small," Kate responded.

"Kate, it's the warmest sweatshirt in the house. Now sit up and put it on," ordered Ravenwood.

Kate obediently sat up, held out her arms and slid into the sweatshirt. As predicted, the sleeves were too long. Also as predicted, it was too small, but that was a perspective thing. The sweatshirt cradled her breasts tightly and snugged around her waist, showing off her body to a striking degree. Kate was not comfortable with the display.

"Too small," she said again, and peeled off the sweatshirt, throwing it directly at Ravenwood's head. He caught the sweatshirt easily and, with a smile flicking at the corner of his mouth, asked whose clothes she would like to try on next.

"Yours," she said succinctly.

"Now, honey. It's going to hang to your knees and we may never get the sleeves rolled up far enough," objected Ravenwood.

"Will it keep me warm?" asked Kate.

"Yes." It was a short reply, no mistaking its sincerity. Whatever else might happen on this adventure, she would not be cold.

Mr. Po tucked her blanket a little higher and busied himself in the kitchen. Ravenwood went to find her a shirt and Brynna came in to keep her awake.

"Da says you can't go to sleep. Mama, Da says you can't go to sleep. You might not wake up!" Brynna was practically bouncing with anguish as Kate started to drift off.

"Calm yourself, Brynna. I promised him I would try to stay awake" assured Kate.

"Are you really trying," asked Brynna?

"Yes, I am really trying," replied Kate.

"Are you sure" asked Brynna, skepticism dripping from her tiny frame.

Now it was Kate's turn to smile. She assured Bryn that she would continue to stay awake. How bright and sparkling she looked there in the kitchen. How Kate wanted to hold her close and tell her everything

11

was fine. What an odd impulse that was. She was not maternal by nature and had only met this child a few hours earlier. Moreover, why was she calling her mama? Bryn had been calling her mama ever since she arrived with the children. How very odd.

Ravenwood returned with a sweater that, as promised, fell to her knees. It was warm, it was soft, and it made Kate very happy.

As Bryn bounced back to the main room, Kate said to Ravenwood, "You really have to get Bryn to stop calling me Mama."

"Why," he asked as he helped her off the counter.

Kate looked at him dazedly for a few moments before she decided it was a serious question, and then responded, "Because I am not her mother, I have no experience being a mother, and her real mother would probably be upset if she heard her – where is her mother anyway? I haven't seen any other women since I got here."

"Brynna's birth mother is dead. I take it you have no children of your own," responded Ravenwood.

"No. I've never had children," said Kate. Ravenwood, looking intently at her face, asked, "And no man either?"

Kate looked somewhat startled at the directness of the question, but asked one of her own. "You mean a permanent, full time man?"

"Yes, that would be the one," said Ravenwood.

"No," said Kate softly. A look passed briefly over her face; some strange brew of loneliness and regret. It was gone almost before Ravenwood registered it was there and Kate said again, "No man of my own."

"What happens next?" asked Kate.

"Supper," replied Mr. Po.

"Supper?" queried Kate.

"Supper," replied Mr. Po emphatically.

Ravenwood picked her up and carried her toward the Living Room just as she was beginning to ask if she could help.

'Mr. Po explained a long time ago, that mostly when we try to help, we are just really in the way. He's very organized and very efficient. We usually just let him go at his own pace," said Ravenwood. He tucked her into a large chair in the Living Room and told the children to make sure she did not fall asleep.

"Weren't there more people here before?" suddenly asked Kate. "Where did they go?"

"One of the mares is ready to foal. They went to the barn to help," explained Ravenwood.

"How could they even find the barn?" wondered Kate aloud.

"We make sure the markers along the drive are good. We check them every fall," explained Luc.

"Then we run a rope through them just to make sure they can be followed," added Trist.

"That way the chores can get done and no one gets lost."

Her eyes moved from boy to boy as they spoke and she began to feel like an observer at a fast tennis match, or maybe ping pong, since they were both bouncing slightly as they talked. They needed to go, to move on, and to expend some of their energy. She understood this. Their heels had begun to bounce. It was time to move.

"Go on," she said to them. "Your heels are bouncing. You need to be moving. I understand that."

"Da said to keep you awake. He understands needing to move, but says we need to learn to control it before it controls us," volunteered Trist.

"He's very big on control," added Luc, "especially self control."

"How do you know about our heels bouncing? I've never thought of it that way, but it's especially right," said Trist. "Do your heels bounce sometimes?'

"They used to. I'm not sure if they will now," replied Kate.

"Sure they will," said Luc. You feel bad now, but that will change. Mr. Po is a wonderful doctor. He has potions for everything."

This made Kate smile. Mr. Po's Potions – sounded like a name for a miracle cure you purchased over the internet.

As promised, the boys continued to talk with her until Mr. Po announced supper. All the children filed through the Dining Room, filling their bowls with stew and settling down on the floor to eat. They heard the side door open, followed by voices and soon Jamie appeared from the Mud Room. The Mud Room connected the porch to the kitchen. It was quite large, contained a full shower, and stacks of clean towels – stacks and stacks of clean towels. Jamie had already taken a quick shower and currently wore nothing except one of the clean towels wrapped around his hips – sort of.

He assured them that the mare and the new foal, nice little stud he called him, were fine and moving nicely. Then he headed upstairs for clothes. This process repeated with Joe and Jonas, Gully and Charlie. Kate waited for more men to appear. Kind of like the small car at the circus, the Mud Room just kept sending men out into the house; nice men, each one wearing nothing but a towel, and none too concerned about whether the towel stayed put or not as they headed up the stairs.

About the time the male review ended, Ravenwood moved her in by the table. She watched in fascination as Mr. Po rolled a loaded cart to the end of the table and began to set out pots of stew, stacks of bowls, spoons, glasses, and water – all from that one spot at the end of the table. She thought of it as the end of the table, but in truth, the table was round. It was at least 10 feet across and the center spun like a built in lazy Susan. The next ring out from the center also spun and was not wood like the rest of the table, but some sort of heat resistant material. It was to this ring that Mr. Po was adding all the food, dishes, and tools, spinning it as he went. How ingenious and how beautiful was the table.

Everyone reappeared, dressed, and hungry, and took seats at the table. As the ring spun, bowls and glasses, spoon and plates moved off to individual place settings until the only vessels left on the ring were the stew and the bread and pitchers of water. Another spin and the bowls and glasses filled, the bread buttered, and supper began. It all happened with no fuss and little effort, almost like magic. Of course, she had taken a hard whack to the head so many things seemed like magic, but it was close.

"Wherever did you get this wondrous table?" asked Kate.

"Gully and Charlie built it," replied Joe. "They have a little shop on the south side of the valley where they make all handmade furniture; even started a small company."

"What's it called?" asked Kate.

"Salt and Gull," replied Gully.

"What does Salt and Gull stand for?" Kate asked.

"Charlie Salt, Ian Gull," explained Jonas. "They just call it Salt and Gull. It's doing pretty well for a small startup."

Fussing suddenly came from the Main Room and Jonas went to check out the problem. Kate looked at her bowl of stew, but had no hunger. She should be hungry; she knew that, but she wasn't, had not been since they arrived.

"You need to eat, Kate," said Ravenwood. "You won't heal and get stronger if you don't eat."

"I'm just not hungry," said Kate with a sigh.

"Eat anyway," he responded tersely.

Dipping her head and sliding her eyes over Ravenwood sitting next to her, she knew that his next response would be to feed her. She just really couldn't deal with that, so she picked up her spoon and dipped it in the stew. She wasn't sure how hot it was so she tentatively touched her tongue to the small bite that she balanced on her spoon. It was warm, but not hot and she took the bite into her mouth, chewing slowly.

"This is wonderful, Mr. Po," said Kate sincerely.

"Mr. Po is the best cook in the west," said Jamie. "We're really lucky he's here, since none of the rest of us is much good at all."

"You can all do the basics. You will never starve," said Mr. Po calmly.

Everyone was enthusiastically devouring the stew; most were on their second helping, some of their third. Kate looked around the table; such a collection she thought. How did these men arrive in the same place? Moreover, they all got along. She was sure it wasn't just surface behavior. She felt something deep and strong moving among these men. She could not put a name to it, but she felt it.

"Do I need to feed you," asked Ravenwood abruptly?

"No," Kate's response was just as abrupt. A few more spoonfuls entered her mouth, but slowly.

"This bowl is too big," she announced.

"Is that your way of saying you're full," asked Ravenwood?

"Yes," replied Kate, nodding her head.

"Just a few more bites," said Ravenwood, "and then you can stop."

Kate obediently dipped her spoon, although she muttered almost nonstop. They couldn't quite make out all the words, but were fairy certain it has something to do with overbearing, arrogant men, bossing her around. The next time she announced the bowl was too big and laid down her spoon, Ravenwood let it go without argument, even though she had eaten less than 10 mouthfuls of the stew and a couple bites of bread.

Mr. Po brought back his cart. As everyone finished eating, the dishes moved back onto the ring that circled the lazy Susan. Mr. Po moved the dishes from the ring to the cart, rolling it back to the kitchen and the clearing up completed. It still felt like magic. She also really wanted a cigarette. She hadn't seen anyone smoke, but maybe no one had the habit. Well, she would have to ask.

"Don't suppose any of you have a cigarette," she asked without much hope.

"Actually, we favor cigars," said Joe, "Much more satisfying. You ever had a cigar"?

"We usually take them on the porch," explained Ravenwood.

They adjourned to the porch, out of the wind. There was a blizzard after all. She was so tired everything seemed like a dream and her head hurt a lot. She was beyond tired, beyond exhausted.

"No, not inhale," said Ravenwood.

"What?" Asked Kate as Ravenwood was lighting her cigar.

"Puff, but do not inhale. It's much stronger than a cigarette. Just let the flavor roll around in your mouth."

There were a few mistakes. She turned a little green, but eventually she found the rhythm. There was much laughter and teasing as she learned what they all seemed to know so naturally. Very few women in the mountains smoked cigars or a pipe. They decided she was a distinct improvement on the usual image. Fortunately, the cigars were slim and almost elegant, not the large, fat stogies everyone thought of. These smelled like some kind of fruitwood, not cherry, apple – that was it, cured with Apple wood. It took her back to her childhood and she began to drift. Her father had smoked cigarettes all the time and a pipe just sometimes; a pipe filled with cherry tobacco. Mom had hated it, that pipe. She would have hated a cigar too. She never complained about the cigarettes. It was funny since she never smoked. They passed drinks to go with the cigars, mostly Bourbon. Kate passed on the offers. She had stopped drinking years ago when alcohol reacted badly with one of her medications. She had since stopped that medicine, in fact had stopped all her meds, but never found a reason to start drinking again. Sometimes she missed a glass of wine with a good dinner, but it was fleeting. Besides, she was wonky enough without the booze, especially now that her head was broken.

Cigars lasted longer than cigarettes, a lot longer. They were a leisurely smoke and no one hurried through them. As she looked round the porch, she tried to remember the relationships among the group. They all related in some way to Ravenwood: father, son, grandson, daughter, and friends. It all radiated like a wheel with him at the center. That image formed in her head. Where was Mr. Po? Didn't he smoke?

"Kate, wake up now. You fall asleep with a cigar in your hand and you'll burn down the house," said Ravenwood.

"House is stone," responded Kate, but rousing herself from the state in which she drifted.

"The outside is rock, carved out of the mountain and snugged down tight. You can call it stone if you want to, but its rock," explained Joe.

"Is there a difference between stone and rock," inquired Gully?

"No idea" responded Joe. "But this rock lives in the mountains. We just borrowed it for a while and built a nice place to live. Took us a while, but we built a nice place."

He stood looking over the porch rail toward the back of the yard. "Once it stops snowing, I'll need to clear a path outside. She's bound to be lonely by now. It's been days since I spoke to her."

"She - who is bound to be lonely" asked Kate?

"Sara, my late wife, I visit her grave most evenings. I know I can talk to her anytime, but she always seems more present at the grave," explained Joe without embarrassment.

"How long has she been gone," asked Kate politely?

"18 months last week," replied Joe.

"It's still fresh then, the loss. I'm so sorry. Is there a picture of her," asked Kate?

Jamie stepped into the Living Room and brought back a framed picture of a lovely woman. Her hair was black and straight. Her eyes were black and bright. Her smile was dazzling, not just because of the contract between her teeth and the light copper of her skin, but something that radiated from inside.

As Kate gazed at the picture, she realized she had been wrong about Ravenwood. He bore such a strong resemblance to his father that it was hard to see anyone else there, until you held the picture of his mother. The coloring was actually hers: Black for the hair, black for the eyes, creamy copper for the skin – a lovely woman, a lovely man – except for that scar that curved across his cheekbone. As scars went, it was not bad, just a smooth white line arching across his face. It must be an old scar and well-taken care of to have healed so cleanly. It rather made him look like a pirate, that and the thick braid of hair that fell to his waist.

She was drifting again and babbling inside her head. It was just in her head wasn't it?

She placed the picture down carefully on the table. Her hand trembled with fatigue. "She was a lovely woman, Joe, just lovely," said Kate.

"Aye, she was that, but more than that," replied Joe.

"More than that?" questioned Kate. "What do you mean – more than that?"

"She was a good looking woman, sure, and she passed these looks along to the boys, but she was the strongest woman I ever knew. It radiated from inside her, that strength. You remind me of her. The same strength radiates from you."

Kate looked slightly stunned. "Thank you, Joe. You are very kind." Joe made a sound somewhere between a grunt and a snort.

"Kindness has no to do with it," said Joe.

"I don't feel very strong right now," protested Kate.

"It's been a rough day," said Ravenwood. "You'll be ruling the house soon."

"Oh, I don't think so," protested Kate.

"Aye, you will," agreed the men, nodding for emphasis as they smoked their cigars.

Kate had been sharing Ravenwood's cigar, and he obligingly offered her another puff. She cupped his hand while she drew on the cigar and she thought again, this is a hard man. He was kind in his own way. He had been taking care of her since she arrived. He did what needed doing, but he took no pleasure in her discomfort. He was tall and well muscled, long muscles, not bunched like a lifter. A body type her mother would have called rangy: wide at the shoulders, lean at the hip, lean all over. There was not an ounce of fat anywhere on him. Come to that, none of them carried anything extra, not the children, and certainly not the men.

As she looked around the porch, she saw much variety in the faces, but only one look. It was a look of respect, acceptance, and relief. That made no sense. Still, that is what she felt on that porch. She was about to begin asking questions. She compulsively asked questions when she didn't understand something, when one of the children appeared at the door.

"Mama Kate, Mama Kate where are you," cried the child?

18

How very odd, thought Kate. What was the matter with the child and why was she calling her Mama Kate?

Jamie stepped over and opened the door, cigar in hand, and the little girl immediately announced, "Smoking is so bad for you. It will kill you."

"Right" said Jamie. "What do you need, Sylvie?"

"I need to see Mama Kate," Sylvie replied stoutly. She marched out onto the porch, looking round until she spotted her objective, then hurried to the side of Kate's chair.

"Are you all right, Mama Kate?" whispered Sylvie frantically.

"Sylvie, my head is broken, my hip is bruised, and I can't go to sleep for fear I will not wake up," stated Kate calmly. "How are you doing?"

Sylvie just stood there staring up at Kate, eyes wide, mouth slightly open, no more words, no more whispers.

"Darling, do go back into the house with the other children and try to get some sleep. Things will look better in the morning, I'm sure," said Kate.

"Yes ma'am," replied Sylvie and headed back through the door.

"What so urgently needed your attention?" asked Gully.

"I've really no idea. Something about Bobby hiding in the closet," said Kate vaguely. An odd look passed along the porch, questioning, but not alarmed.

As everyone finished their cigar, they drifted back into the house, which slowly quieted.

"Why are the floors so warm?" asked Kate suddenly.

"There is a hot spring in the mountain behind us. We use it for hot water all year, but in winter, we also run it through pipes in the foundation. We don't even need fires most of the time, just small ones in the morning or evening. Of course, blizzards are an exception and we keep the fires going, especially with all the children here. Most of the time it's not required, but it is a comfort," explained Ravenwood. "Still, bed is the warmest, most comfortable place for the night." With that, he picked her up and carried her up the stairs to the second floor.

"What are we doing now?" asked Kate.

"Going to bed," replied Ravenwood, opening a door to a bedroom and sitting her softly on the bed.

"Jamie has found you a t-shirt to wear if you're inclined to pajamas. The bathroom is here in the corner. Can you manage by yourself while I check the upstairs fires?" explained Ravenwood.

"Yes, I can manage, thank you," responded Kate with some asperity.

"No sleeping. Keep moving until I get back," ordered Ravenwood.

"No sleeping," agreed Kate. She was not accustomed to constantly being around people, having spent most of her adult life alone, and she began to chafe under the restrictions and attention, but there was always someone watching, watching over. Being watched over gave her such a grand feeling. There was always someone looking out for her safety, making sure she didn't get overtired and careless. It gave her such a feeling of security and peace. Not just Ravenwood watched over her, although it began with him. The entire family did their part. She was never alone, not really. Someone was always near, to help and to protect. It took her a long time to recognize this and even longer to adjust. It started when she arrived in the valley, when Ravenwood carried her into the house and Brynna took her hand. Luc and Trist immediately fell into line, having cared for her when she fell and directing her home.

She draped the t-shirt over the walker and headed for the bathroom, only to stop about half way there. A walker: where did this walker come from and why had no one brought it down earlier? As she continued on to the bathroom, she got her answer. Even with the walker, movement was difficult, and so very painful. When she reached the bathroom, she found her kit with all her cleansers and lotions and potions sitting proudly on top of the commode. She could have sworn she left that by the road when they had to make room for John Paul. She left pretty much everything by the side of the road as she tucked kids into her car, but here it was - more magic.

She heard the bedroom door open, close, and wood dropping into the wood box, but concentrated on doing a thorough job of cleansing her face. It had been a stressful day. A shower would feel good. She wasn't sure she could stand that long, but the walker would help and she was just about to take the plunge when Ravenwood knocked on the door and asked if she was all right. She finally responded to his question. It felt like hours since he asked it.

"I'm fine, just slow - very slow."

"Good. Mister Po says we need to massage more of his liniment into your hip, try to get the blood collected under the skin moving away."

Kate opened the door and began her awkward limp toward the bed. It was hard to watch. It was obviously painful. It would have been so much easier for him to pick her up, but he did not and she made her way slowly to the side of the bed. Painful as it was to watch, he knew the only way she would get better was to push.

As she lowered herself to sit on the side of the bed, he reached for her with an arm under her knees and the other across her back. He lay her down and rolled her onto her right side.

"This bed is very hard," announced Kate.

"Hmgph," was the only response.

She found a pillow and wrapped her arms around it, pulling it close against her chest as Ravenwood bent her left knee and swept the t-shirt up and away, leaving her hip bare. He eased down on the bed beside her, rubbing his hands with the liniment, warming them with the friction. Kate was trembling as he began to work the lotion over her hip and leg.

"Take it easy now, Kate. This won't take long. I've never seen a bruise quite this bad," said Ravenwood.

"It's dark and angry," replied Kate, squirming as he moved his hands.

He was surprisingly gentle. The hands glided in a soothing rhythm. He was careful not to press too hard, so very careful. She almost cried out a few times. The bruise stretched from her waist to her knee, darker in some of the places. She would not be without pain for several weeks, perhaps longer.

He felt her body relax and knew she was drifting toward sleep.

"Talk to me, Kate. Talk to me so I know you are awake," requested Ravenwood. Of course, it sounded more like an order, but she knew it was a request. "I don't have so much to say," said Kate.

Now he looked at her with a surprised smile, and this time he asked, "How did you know my given name?"

"Your what?" Kate asked.

"How did you know my first name, my given name? No one uses it since my mother died. How did you know it was Jacob?" asked Ravenwood.

"What else would it be?" Kate replied cryptically.

"Could be anything," responded Ravenwood.

"No. It needed to be Jacob," said Kate as she drifted almost to sleep.

Ravenwood made no further comment. It would not do to make her angry. He had been searching for her for such a long time. She was hurt now, but she would heal. Her hip would get better, he corrected. Her head was anybody's guess. She described it as broken, but he didn't think that was accurate. After all, she rescued a busload of kids from freezing to death in a freak blizzard and got them all here safely. That was after the cosh on the head. The head must not be working too badly.

He stopped the massage with a pat and a caution to let the liniment sink in before she covered up.

"Easy for you to say - it's cold up here," said Kate.

"You won't freeze," replied Ravenwood as he went to the bathroom to wash.

Kate did not wait long to pull down the t-shirt and tuck the blanket in around herself. She was cold. She knew the house was warm enough. It was not her skin that was too cool. She called it cold from the inside out. It happened sometimes. Usually it meant she needed something to eat or she needed to sleep. It was obvious which one she needed now, but Ravenwood was determined to keep her awake. He was such a stubborn man!

The stubborn man came out of the bathroom and began to undress. Kate watched him with interest and apprehension. All the lights were out now, but the glow from the fire lit the room softly. She felt the bed move as Ravenwood eased down on the side. He had pulled back the blankets from that side of the bed and stretched like some large beast there.

"Kate, you're not talking," chided Ravenwood.

"Are you naked?" asked Kate.

Ravenwood gave out a sharp crack of laughter. She felt his body convulse and the bed jerk. He was not accustomed to laughter. Kate could tell he was rusty.

"I never learned to sleep all wrapped up and bound," replied Ravenwood, the humor still lacing his voice.

"Don't you get cold?" asked Kate.

"No."

"I get cold sometimes, so very cold," said Kate.

Ravenwood rolled to his left side and raised himself on one elbow. There was a tension in him now. Intervention and distraction were required. She was beginning to panic. Panic never helped. She needed to remain calm. Of course, anger could be helpful. Anger could be very helpful, but she didn't think he would respond well to anger. Curiosity would be better. She was good at questions, yes, curiosity was better.

"Ravenwood, what are you doing in my bed?" asked Kate. The laughter began as a rumble in his chest and exploded outward to bounce off the walls. Like some kind of wave that had crashed here in the room, it eddied round her, finally flowing back into the still water.

Downstairs, the men looked at each other in shock. Ravenwood never laughed aloud like that. A smile, a chuckle, a bit of sarcasm – that they had all seen and heard – but this was different, very different.

"As you looked around the room, did you see anything familiar?" asked Ravenwood of Kate once he had stopped laughing – mostly stopped. He was still amused.

"No, nothing is familiar. I just arrived today. How could anything be familiar?" replied Kate in some confusion.

"That's kind of my point," said Ravenwood calmly. "It's my room and my bed."

"Oh, good point," said Kate.

She tilted her head and considered this information - his house, his room, his bed.

Ravenwood, what am I doing in your bed?" asked Kate. Again, the laughter cracked through the room. Again, the men downstairs looked up at the ceiling in amazement.

"I think that's probably a good sign," said Joe. "She's making him laugh; spooky, but good, I think."

"Never heard him laugh like that before," said Gully. "I've known him for a long time. This is different."

"Like I said, it's maybe a good thing," added Joe. The card game downstairs continued. The children asleep in the Main Room continued. The strange conversation in the upstairs bedroom continued.

"Right at the moment, not too much, but I have hopes for when your hip is healed," Ravenwood answered her question bluntly.

"Hmgph," she responded, prompting another laugh from Ravenwood.

"It didn't take long to pick up that expression," he observed.

"It's a good sound, just difficult to spell," said Kate.

Ravenwood arched a brow and looked at her quizzically. Why would you care how to spell it? He had heard and used it all his life. He had never even tried to spell it. Ah -– Diversion, damn she was good!

"If you have an objection to this bed, there are several available – some older, some younger, some much younger. You can probably take your pick," volunteered Ravenwood.

Now it was Kate's turn to look at him in confusion: some older, some younger, some much younger.

"Beds do not usually have ages like people," said Kate.

"That is true," agreed Ravenwood.

Kate continued to look at him in confusion, trying to figure out what he was offering her: some older, some younger, some much younger. Oh, she really had taken a hard knock to the head. Why, was he, how did he think she, oh that had to be it. He was not offering her a choice of beds. He was offering her a choice of men: some older, some younger, some much younger. Was that right? That was so bizarre. Why would he offer her a choice of men? The tension radiating from him was almost a physical thing.

"I like this bed," said Kate quietly.

Ravenwood continued to look intently into her eyes for several more seconds. It felt like minutes, it could have been hours. Now the tension that held him so rigid began to drain away.

"Good," he said succinctly.

Ravenwood slid under the blanket on his side of the bed, leaving the quilts folded over on top of Kate. Was he finally growing cold? Kate soon realized that was not the case. Heat radiated from his side of the bed. It drew her like the proverbial magnet. She tucked herself against his side, her head resting on his shoulder. As she lapped up the warmth, her hand found and traced the scars that covered his side. Without thinking, she said, "Ravenwood, such pain, what caused you such pain?"

"Its old pain, honey," said Ravenwood.

"The body remembers. Its memory is separate from the one in your head," explained Kate.

He looked at her seriously for a few seconds and then said, "You have a different perspective on many things. Has it always been that way?"

"Sort of, but I think getting whacked on the head exaggerated the problem," said Kate.

"Exacerbated the problem?" asked Ravenwood.

"Whichever. It made it bigger, more noticeable, harder to control," said Kate.

"You do know that the phrase 'getting whacked on the head' implies that someone hit you, not that you hit something," explained Ravenwood.

"What phrase would you prefer?" Kate asked sarcastically.

"There's the woman who told me I couldn't undress her in the kitchen," said Ravenwood.

"A lot of good that did me," grumbled Kate, shifting her position against him; at least she tried to shift her position. With his arm clamped around her waist, she did not have much wiggle room

"What are you doing?" Ravenwood asked mildly.

Kate looked somewhat stricken, somewhat embarrassed, and hesitant to say what the problem was. As Ravenwood continued to wait for an answer, she finally gave it up.

"I have to pee," she said with a deep sigh.

Ravenwood swung out of bed, scooped her up, and carried her to the bathroom, ignoring her protests as he went.

"You can't take me to the bathroom. I am not going to pee with you there. Really, Ravenwood, a person needs a little privacy."

As he sat her on top of the closed toilet saying, "Holler when you are finished," he left the bathroom and closed the door behind him.

Well, that was exasperating. She couldn't even get angry with him. As she finished with the bathroom, she opened the door and made her way slowly toward the bed. Her hip had begun to stiffen. The stiffness did not take long to set in, so she continued moving slowly. Ravenwood watched, but did not move until she approached the bed.

"This bed is too tall," said Kate.

"Depends on how tall you are," replied Ravenwood.

"It needs a stool in front of it," argued Kate.

"That, we can do," said Ravenwood, laying her softly on the bed and pulling the quilts up around her.

As he climbed into bed, Kate rolled over against his side. How natural it was to hold her, to feel her breathe. She must have felt something similar. His thigh supported her left leg, bent at the knee. Her arms were around his waist, her head against his chest. The body remembers. Wasn't that what she said? Yes, the body remembers.

They talked gently through the night. Ravenwood made the rounds to check the fires. She tried hard to stay awake, but usually drifted off before he returned.

By morning, the sharing and deciding were complete. They were together and they would stay together. Kate had never moved so quickly in any relationship. They did not speak of love, for that did not define it. It was a knowing; deep inside, that they were better together.

The room became brighter – sort of – and Kate could see the style. In her head, she named it 'Early American Spartan'. There was nothing extra, no frills, no flounces, and no softness. Even the mattress where they lay was hard and she began to shift to find comfort.

"Kate, what are you doing," inquired Ravenwood?

"This mattress is too hard," said Kate. "It has no softness, no comfort."

"Then we might as well take a shower," said Ravenwood, climbing out of bed.

The abrupt change of topic did not seem to throw Kate, who rolled to the edge of the bed, sat up, and asked, "Do we know what the time is?"

"Why would we care," countered Ravenwood.

"Good point," conceded Kate as Ravenwood once again carried her into the bathroom.

It was very domestic, being in the bathroom with him. The bathroom was not small. It must have been another room and converted during a house upgrade.

Kate pulled up her hair and began to wash her face. Ravenwood looked on with fascination as she wound the length of her hair round her hand, anchoring it on top of her head with what looked like large colorful bugs.

As Ravenwood squeezed the ends of the bug, pieces of hair began to escape. When he pulled it loose, the knot of hair slid sideways and was in danger of toppling altogether.

"What is this," asked Ravenwood?

"That is a hair-clippie-thing," replied Kate helpfully.

"Hmgph," was the only reply, but he handed back the hair clippie thing so she could anchor her hair.

He turned on the shower and warm air began to flow around them.

"Ravenwood, I'm not really sure I'm ready for this," said Kate hesitantly. "I don't usually shower with someone until after I've gotten to know them, and we just...." Her voice trailed off as Ravenwood opened the shower door. It was a large shower and it looked wonderfully soothing.

Soothing went out the window as Ravenwood peeled her t-shirt off over her head and, wrapping his hands around her waist, lifted her into the shower with him. "That takes care of that," said Ravenwood.

A long sensuous moan came from Kate as the warm water snaked down her body, "Ohhhh." There were showerheads at both ends of the booth and the water arched together, hitting her skin from every angle. This was surprising. This was wonderful. She might never leave this little booth with the lovely water.

"Kate, you keep moaning and moving like that and I'm going to totally forget that your hip is badly injured and needs to heal," warned Ravenwood flatly.

"It feels so good," said Kate smiling. "How can just plain water feel so good?"

Ravenwood turned his back and began to soap himself. Within minutes, he was done and climbing out of the shower. Reaching for a towel, he slung it around his hips and turned back to Kate, who was currently washing her hair.

He watched her through the shower doors as she lifted and rinsed that mass of curls, flipping it over and rinsing it down to get the soap completely out, wrapping it securely in a towel when she was done. Of course, the towel was not big enough and the hair trailed out the end of the wrap. He was familiar with that. With a last rinse of her body, she exited the shower, reaching for a towel. He wrapped her securely in a towel, patting her parts under the pretext of drying her off. She had some very nice parts.

"Should I pat you down and check you out?" asked Kate.

"Sure," replied Ravenwood, tugging loose the towel and spreading his arms to give her clear access.

His hard-on was enormous. She had never seen one so large. Of course, she hadn't seen all that many. It had been years since she saw a man naked, longer since she touched one, even longer since she allowed herself to be touched. Ravenwood wrapped the towel back around his hips and then finished briskly patting Kate dry.

Sweet was the word to describe her body.

Trim, but not heavily muscled, not skinny, with a nice round ass. That was the word circling Ravenwood's brain as he finished drying Kate. Unconsciously, he gave that nice round ass a gentle squeeze and went to get dressed.

Kate toweled her hair dry and began combing through any tangles. There weren't many. She had brushed her hair the night before so the only tangles left were just the ones from sleeping and washing. She finished her comb through and flipped her hair back just as Ravenwood returned to the bathroom. He regarded her from the doorway. He was a man seeing a vision. There she stood, naked, her curls tumbling over her shoulders, cradling her breasts, just kissing her hips.

Wonder how long it would be until her hip could take the pounding from sex. Maybe if she could be on top it would happen sooner.

"Ravenwood, are you all right?" Kate asked. "You really look a little green."

"Hmgph," replied Ravenwood. "I'll find you some clothes, before I loose what little self-control I have left, thought Ravenwood to himself.

As Kate limped from the bathroom, she lost her balance and nearly fell. Ravenwood caught her tight against his body and rocked her gently to calm them both. That had been close. She didn't need another nasty fall. She was exhausted. Maybe food would help. She had not eaten much the day before. He lifted her and started down the hall to the stairs. Balancing was a little trickier on the way down, but Ravenwood managed easily and they soon entered the kitchen.

All the men had gathered around the table except Charlie. He was checking the fires at the workshop. Keeping a fire going unattended at the shop was a tricky business. The stove there was sound as a tank and Charlie did not spend much time on worry. Still, it was a concern. All the children were still asleep in the Main Room except Luc and Trist, who were having coffee with the men.

"Good morning," said Kate in greeting as Ravenwood walked into the room.

"Morning," they responded.

Mr. Po came to check her responses this morning and she asked how much longer she had to stay awake.

"At least several more hours to be safe," was the reply. She opened her mouth to protest, but Mr. Po was already explaining. "It was evening when you arrived. It must have been past noon when you hit your head. It needs to be at least around noon before you sleep."

"Hmgph," replied Kate to laughter all round.

"It didn't take you long to pick up that expression, Sis" said Joe with affection. She looked at him fixedly across the table, thinking how long it had been since anyone called her Sis. It had been years since her father died. It felt good, Joe calling her Sis, just as her father always had.

"Is something wrong, Kate?" asked Jonas.

"Sleepy," replied Kate.

"Single minded little thing, isn't she?" observed Jonas. Kate tilted her head in what Ravenwood had privately begun to call the defiant puppy dog.

"How very condescending," said Kate, looking directly at Jonas, who immediately looked both surprised and contrite?

"I apologize, Kate. I didn't realize how it would actually sound out loud," said Jonas.

"Now you know why he avoided trial law," said Ravenwood.

"You are a lawyer?" asked Kate with some interest.

"Yes," replied Jonas.

"What kind of law do you practice?'

"Wills, trusts, land sales, that sort of thing," said Jonas.

Kate opened her mouth to ask another question, but Ravenwood laid his hand over hers and said "Jonas handles he legal work for all the various businesses we run out of the valley."

"OK," said Kate slowly, "How many businesses are we talking about?"

"Four," answered Ravenwood.

"Four?" questioned Kate.

"Four," reiterated Ravenwood.

"How fascinating," Kate observed.

"Food first, fascination later," instructed Ravenwood gruffly.

Kate looked at her plate in some confusion. She did not remember adding any food to it, but there it sat, completely loaded. She slid her eyes sideways at Ravenwood as she observed, "This plate is too big."

"Eat," urged Ravenwood with some exasperation.

Kate obediently took a bite, and then another, and was soon happily munching away. She was about half way through the plate of food when she stopped and laid down her fork.

"This was very good, Mr. Po. Thank you," she said politely.

"You haven't eaten much, Sis. How you going to heal up that leg if you don't eat?" asked Joe.

"I ate plenty. The leg will heal. It's the head that will not," said Kate stubbornly.

"Maybe so, maybe not," said Joe. "Either way, we've got stock to take care of."

With that, they got up and began to put on their layers of outdoor clothing. Joe pulled Ravenwood aside for a short chat, and then they were gone down to the barns. Ravenwood returned quickly. He stocked the wood boxes. He checked the house for obvious leaks and then he began to push the heavy snow off the roof, even though the snow continued to fall.

Kate began her exercises to help her leg recover as quickly as possible. It was apparent from the start that the recovery would not be quick and it would not be painless. Kate began simply to walk, to get the blood moving to her injured parts. Even with the cane, movement was difficult. The first day she only moved between the kitchen and Main room three times. Tomorrow she would do better, she said to herself, and tomorrow she did, but that day she fought to stay awake. She thought she had an opportunity for sleep when Ravenwood was busy with the chores, but Mr. Po took over his watch and kept her busy.

Today's meal appeared to be chili, huge pots of chili.

"Mr. Po, this would be really lovely with a big pan of corn bread," observed Kate.

"Yes, it would be," said Mr. PO. "Unfortunately, I do not bake."

"Not bake?" queried Kate.

"I can cook anything, but Joe describes my bread as making a wonderful door stop," explained Mr. PO.

"It's been many years since I did any baking, but it usually turned out just fine. Do you have the ingredients for corn bread?'

"Yes, I have them, but you must not be up on your leg so much," said Mr. Po.

"That's why God invented kitchen stools," replied Kate.

Therefore, they set to work: Kate on a stool, Mr. Po moving between the cabinet and the island. They were making a test batch to make sure the recipe was correct before they made a large batch. Soon the room filled with the smell of baking bread, drawing the children in. Mr. Po set a timer when they put the first pan in the oven. Now Kate checked for doneness.

"Needs another couple minutes," said Kate. "The top should be a nice kind of golden brown."

Removed from the oven and allowed to cool, it was time for the taste test. It passed with flying-colors. The children devoured that pan of corn bread as if it was the best treat they ever had. It was only mid-morning. They had already eaten breakfast, but they slathered that bread with butter and jam and jelly and syrup and they ate until there was nothing but crumbs left in the pan. Then they cleaned up the crumbs.

"We need a much bigger batch," said Kate.

"We need a MUCH bigger batch," agreed Mr. Po. "Wait here." He disappeared down the stairs, but returned in only a few minutes. He then proceeded to unpack and wash a large stand mixer. Kate had always wanted one of these, but never felt justified in spending the money. Wow, it was beautiful.

"How many times do I increase the recipe?" asked Kate. "The recipe in my head makes one small pan of corn bread." Snow slid off the roof right outside the kitchen windows, causing her to jump.

"12 times," said Mr. Po.

"What," asked Kate?

"We need 12 pans of corn bread to get through lunch and supper. The men will probably not return to the house until mid-afternoon or early evening. It's too much effort to get back and forth repeatedly." He explained as more snow hit the ground.

"Do we have enough stuff to make 12 pans of bread?" asked Kate doubtfully.

"Oh, yes," responded Mr. PO.

She decided to mix six pans at a time and set the recipe up accordingly. The mixer really held a lot, and it made the mixing so much easier. As the dough was nearly ready, Kate turned to Mr. Po to asking,

"Do we even have 12 pans to use to bake this?"

"Yes, and we can re-use the pans from the first batch for the second," responded Mr. Po calmly.

"When should we bake these?" We will want at least a couple of them to still be warm when the children are ready to eat."

"Lunch is in about half an hour," said Mr. Po.

"Then we should preheat the oven and bake some bread," said Kate, beginning to move off her stool.

"I will pre-heat the oven. You will check the batter. Yes?"-prompted Mr. Po.

"Yes," replied Kate.

She decided the batter was too thick and began to add water. She added a teaspoon and mixed, added a teaspoon and mixed, until she was satisfied with the consistency. Mr. Po watched this process in fascination. He could make pan gravy to perfection, but he had no feel for this. He stirred the chili. He had 10 quarts of chili. He knew that there would be barely enough left for tomorrows lunch once everyone got through tonight. He wondered how long it would snow this time. He had plenty of food in the pantry and the freezers. They would not starve and they would not freeze - Could be worse. Enough reflection he said to himself. Kate was nodding on her stool.

"Talk to me, Kate," said Mr. Po. Kate snapped awake and began to list to her left. Mr. Po straightened her before she could fall and continued to try to get her to talk. She was exhausted, poor woman. Soon she would be able to sleep as long as she wished. He checked her eyes again just to be sure. Her pupils were equal and reactive; this was good. Mr. Po had never seen Ravenwood react so strongly to a woman; he hovered, he worried, he practically clucked over her. All of this was out of character, to the point of being spooky.

Let's put some bread in to bake," encouraged Mr. Po. Kate had filled the pans and he now slid three of them into the top oven and set the timer on the left side of the over. Then he opened the lower oven and slid in the three remaining pans, setting a separate timer for that oven.

"How many ovens do we have?" asked Kate.

"Just the two," replied Mr. Po. Of course, you can cook a lot of food in 2 ovens."

"That's a very large oven, Mr. Po," observed Kate.

"It's a commercial grade oven. Thought it would last longer, given the size of the family. All the equipment here in the kitchen is commercial grade." He began unthinkingly to wipe the countertops. Maybe he was a little OCD. It didn't really hurt in a kitchen.

"When did you redo the kitchen," asked Kate.

"2, 21/2 years ago," replied Mr. Po.

"Have you always done all the cooking," asked Kate.

"No, Mother Ravenwood cooked. She was a good cook," Mr. Po explained.

"Where is she now?" asked Kate.

"She is buried in the side garden. It's under snow now, but in the spring, the garden is beautiful. Joe finds it very peaceful. He talks to her every night," explained Mr. Po.

"Sounds nice," said Kate.

As the smell of the baking bread mixed with the smell of the simmering chili, it wafted through the house like a siren call. It danced on the nose. It beckoned to the eyes with promises of perfection. It played against the ears: Eat, come and eat, Look what they made for you. Come and eat.

The children ate. Three pans of corn bread and two quarts of chili later, they were at last satisfied.

They were intrigued when Kate taught them to use the cornbread like crackers, crumble it in the bowl and dump the chili over it. Their disappointment over the lack of crackers soon turned to glee as they discovered just how good the mixture was. Mr. Po knew he had crackers, many crackers. He just couldn't remember where he put them. Everywhere he looked, they were not. How do you misplace that many crackers? What happens to them? Does something eat them?

"Mr. Po, how much longer?" asked Kate.

"How much longer, what?" asked Mr. Po.

"How much longer do I have to stay awake?" reiterated Kate?

"Just a few more hours, a few more." assured Mr. Po.

"Need to do something," said Kate, and she began to mix the batter for the rest of the cornbread.

Mr. Po, realizing she was trying hard to stay awake, let her mix and measure, as long as she stayed on her stool, and kept the pressure off her hip. He turned the cornbread out on the counter to cool and began to wash and dry the pans in preparation for the next baking. When everything was in readiness for the next meal, Mr. Po suggested she read to the children. They would enjoy it and it might even put some of them to sleep for a while. He helped her to the Main Room and into a large chair, tucking pillows against her left side for more support.

"Would you children like to hear a story?" asked Kate.

"Yes, are you going to tell us one?" they asked.

"I thought I would read one," replied Kate.

"Better if you tell one. We've heard all the stories in the books. Make us a new one, a story just for us," they urged.

Thinking hard she said, "You must give me the first line," and waited for them to decide.

Trist finally spoke, "The snow fell like rain that winter in the small town of Mt. Olive."

-At first, it covered the streets-, continued Kate, - then it covered the sidewalks. It crept in the doors of the shops and clung to the windows.-

The children were enthralled. It was just a simple story, but they paid attention all the way through and then several of the younger ones laid down for a nap. The rest pulled out books and games to occupy their time. Kate looked around the room carefully. There was no television. How very refreshing. Of course, it could simply be in another room, but she did not think so. The boys moved too easily to games and books for TV to be a habit. It was, after all, much easier just to flip it on.

The snow had stopped its suicide plunge from the roof some time ago and she began to wonder where Ravenwood was. Mr. Po explained there were several buildings that needed the snow pushed off the roof and he had probably moved on to another of them. He would be back for supper, not to worry. There was nothing to do, but wait.

She soon heard the sound of the snowmobile coming up the road and knew that everyone was on the way home. The first to arrive were Jonas and Joe, pausing in the mudroom to undress and grab a quick shower to warm up, Joe entered the kitchen as he finished his shower, steaming and glowing. With a towel around his hips, Joe stopped to take a deep breath.

"Smells wonderful, Mr. Po. Have you been practicing your baking?" asked Joe dubiously.

"No," replied Mr. Po briefly.

Spotting the pans of bread cooled on the counter, he headed up the stairs to dress without another word. As Jonas came out of the shower, he also paused to breathe in the aroma of the baking bread. He stopped to taste a bit from the pan left from lunch.

"Mr. Po, this is really good," Jonas said in surprise, as he reached for another piece, larger this time.

"The children already devoured 3 pans with lunch, so I assumed it was good," Mr. Po commented.

"When did you learn to do this?" asked Jonas as he watched Mr. Po slide 2 more pans of batter into the oven and set another timer.

With a roll of his eyes, followed by a spate of Chinese, Mr. Po again explained that he had not baked the cornbread.

"Then who did?" asked Jonas.

The sounds of Kate moving through the house became audible as she neared the kitchen. It was very distinctive with the thud of the cane and the delay caused by the injured hip. As she rounded the corner from the hall, Mr. Po inclined his head in her direction.

"Cornbread is really good, Kate" Jonas greeted her.

"Thank you," she responded automatically as she looked up and saw Jonas, bare foot and clad only in his towel, reaching for another piece of bread.

He had the same body type as his father; tall, no fat, muscles long and lean, shoulders wide, hips narrow and about to loose the fight to keep the towel in place, and no scars. He was quite altogether lovely. It would have made opting for a younger bed very interesting. Another snowmobile arrived outside, this time with Jamie and Gully. Joe came down from upstairs, spotting Jonas with the cornbread and asked if he was starving or just deranged? Jonas held out a bite of bread to him saying, "You should just taste. It's really good."

"Hmgph," was the only response. Kate laughed merrily at the scene in the kitchen as Jonas tried to convince Joe to taste the cornbread.

"Oh, well, more for me if you don't eat any," said Jonas as he went up the stairs, crossing to his wing of the house.

"When did you take up baking, Mr. Po, asked Joe?

"I gave up on it a long time ago," said Mr. Po.

"Then where did this come from," asked Joe with more than a little curiosity. Again, Mr. Po nodded in Kate's direction.

"She can bake," asked Joe in wonder?

"Apparently so," was the response.

"Been a long time since anyone baked for us," said Joe, thinking back to some of the treats his wife had produced over the years. Some of them had been a success, some a flop, but they were all eaten. It would be the same with Kate. They ate every thing she made. As Sara used to say, "You must show appreciation for my efforts." Wonder what else Kate could bake? Cornbread was relatively basic, but you never knew. Had to be something hidden in the girl. He never saw Ravenwood so drawn to a woman. However, what did he know about his son's taste in women. Ravenwood had been gone from this valley since he joined the marines when he was 18. There was the occasional visit, but those were rare, and never an indication of staying. When his brother died somewhere out west, he went and found the children, gathered them up, and brought them all home. He also brought Mr. Po, Charlie, and Gully. All seemed to be good men and had obviously been with Ravenwood for a long time. Many things had changed since they came to the valley; none for the worse, except his Sara dying, but sickness knows no bounds and that would have happened anyway. Joe had a feeling things were about to change again. That was good.

A woman was the heart of a home. Men could muddle through OK, and they had. The children were well fed and clean and generally healthy, but there was something missing. Brynna had seen it right away with Kate. The children all craved her touch, arching and preening like small wild animals waiting for their mother's grooming. Soon they would recognize her as their mother, just as they recognized Ravenwood as their father. Soon Kate would recognize they were her children, whether she had birthed them or not. Now, Ravenwood had to make her want to stay. Oh, he could make her stay, but he had to make her want to stay. Everything was going well so far, but that might all change once the blizzard was over. They only had a short window.

Jamie and Gully were the next to arrive at the house. The showers were quick, but warm, and their mouths were watering by the time they hit the kitchen.

Kate was looking out the window in between trips to exercise her leg. It was the very definition of a blizzard, snowing and blowing. Would it never stop?

"Wow," said Jamie." This is good cornbread. When is supper?"

"When we all get home safe we'll eat," replied Joe. "Go get dressed."

Jamie, as seemed to be the habit with the Ravenwoods, had on nothing but a towel following his shower. Gully emerged clad just the same. She began to wonder if the towels were normal or just for her. How many towels would they go through if they did this every night? It would be less if they kept track of their towel and reused them rather than tossing them in the laundry. After all, towels did not need washing after every use. Contrary to some people's belief, they were not 'dirty' just because they were used to dry clean water from your clean body or your clean hair. This was an important concept to grasp when you had grown up using communal towels. She still remembered the first time she learned about individual towels, how each person had their own towel that they brought with them to the bathroom and then returned it to their room to dry. It was from a TV show, you now the one where they had all the kids and lived on a mountain. Funny what you learned from TV.

She heard the snowmobile, Charlie and Ravenwood entering the mudroom, and the shower start almost simultaneously. She knew these things could not all be happening at the same time, but that's the way it seemed in her head. Then they were sitting down to supper, the chili and cornbread disappearing as if inhaled. Where did it go, exactly? The lazy Susan went round, the bowls filled, emptied, and filled again. It was a good thing they had baked so many pans of bread. Kate was so fascinated with watching the process that she forgot to eat until Ravenwood reminded her.

"You need to eat, Kate."

"I've been eating."

"Sure, and that's why your bowl is still full."

"It's a magic bowl. No matter how much you eat, it's just still full."

"Right, and here I was thinking it was full because you hadn't eaten a thing. Let's test it, shall we? Have a big bite," said Ravenwood ladling up a spoonful of chili.

He fed her several spoonfuls of chili while they waited for the bowl. It did not refill of course, but he managed to get about half a bowl down her before she conceded that it was not magic.

Then Mr. Po was checking her eyes, feeling her head, and telling her she could sleep if she wanted to. What an odd way to phrase it, if she wanted to. She was practically falling asleep on the table. Her body was so tired.

"Kate, should I take you upstairs," asked Ravenwood? She nodded her head and lifted her arms to indicate she was ready and he picked her up. As he went rapidly up the stairs, he cradled her firmly against his chest. That felt so good; to hold her hard against his body, to feel her breathe, to feel her heartbeat. Yes, it felt good.

As they reached the bedroom, Ravenwood helped her change into the t-shirt she was using for a nightgown and tucked her snugly into the bed. How long would he have the pleasure he wondered? A very long time, he replied firmly, a very long time.

"Ravenwood, are you coming to bed?" asked Kate?

"I realize you need to sleep, honey, but it's too early in the evening for me. It's barely 6 o'clock," replied Ravenwood.

"Are you coming to bed later," asked Kate, not to be deterred?

"Yes, I will come to bed later. I'll try not to wake you, but no guarantees."

"I do not need guarantees. I have no worry that you will wake me," assured Kate.

Ravenwood simply lifted her hand and kissed her palm in answer and that made her smile.

"Now, go to sleep," ordered Ravenwood. She giggled. Someone couldn't just go off to sleep because of an order.

"Will you stay until I sleep?" asked Kate.

"Yes," he replied, stroking her hair.

"Can I sleep as long as I want?" she asked as her words began to slur.

"As long as you want," he assured her.

With that exchange, she was asleep.

Ravenwood lingered a few minutes just to make sure, but she was definitely asleep. He wondered how long she would sleep and thought it would be through the night. He would check on her frequently this evening. He really couldn't help it. The compulsion to make sure she was safe was too strong.

When Ravenwood finally came to bed, he entered the room quietly, leaving it mostly in darkness Kate curled on her right side, still sleeping deeply. He undressed and slid into the bed and – where was his pillow? He checked the bed. He checked the floor around the bed. He even checked under the bed. It couldn't just disappear. It had been here earlier in the evening. As he lay back on the bed to think about the possibilities, he slid his arm around Kate's shoulders. She huddled close, seeking his warmth and there between them was the missing pillow. She had been clutching it tightly to her chest. He did not know why exactly, but she had released it and now wrapped her arms around him - much better. He tucked the pillow behind his head and went to sleep.

He woke early in the morning. Kate still curled against him; her head on his shoulder, her knee braced across his thigh, she showed no sign of having moved since he came to bed. He felt good, holding her like this. He felt peaceful, how long had it been since he felt this way. For a while, he simply lay there feeling good. He heard the morning sounds of the house, but felt no urge to join in yet.

He heard Mr. Po in the kitchen. He heard his father in the bathroom. He heard the children in the Main Room, already squabbling and fussing. What time was it? 0930. He could not remember the last time he was still in bed at 0930. He slid his hand around Kate's throat to check her pulse and was surprised when she nuzzled him. Her pulse was strong and even. He really wanted to wake her, but he had promised she could sleep as long as she wanted. He had to get up before his cock exploded. He had never been so hard, so frequently. Sliding carefully out of the bed, he tucked another quilt around Kate and went into the bathroom. By the time he came out to get dressed, his pillow was already gone. Having learned from last night's experience, he flipped back the quilts and, sure enough, she had it wrapped tightly in her arms. How interesting! She hadn't moved a muscle in hours, but as soon as he left the bed, she found his pillow and … -He really didn't want to think about this anymore. He finished dressing, grabbed his shoes, and headed out the door, where he collided firmly with Joe.

Joe would have fallen, but Ravenwood's arms shot out to steady him. "Just like running into a wall," muttered Joe.

"The wall would have let you fall on your ass," responded Ravenwood.

"Hmgph," was the only reply from Joe.

"What brings you around this morning?" asked Ravenwood.

"Never seen you sleep so late. Thought something might be wrong. Got tired of fielding questions about it from the children," replied Joe.

"I promised her she could sleep as long as she wanted. Her pulse is strong and steady. I really don't want to wake her unless Mr. Po says it's important," said Ravenwood.

"That's the longest speech I've heard you give in the last 3 years," said Joe, heading down the stairs.

The odd smile kicked up the corner of Ravenwood's mouth briefly as he followed his father down the stairs.

The children were practically bouncing off the walls in the Main Room, having had their breakfast some time ago. Charlie, Jamie, Jonas, and Gully were gone to feed the stock. He grabbed a cup of coffee and walked out on the porch. Mr. Po kept the coffee hot and strong all day. It was good, especially on a morning like this. There was not even a hint of sunshine. Snow fell sideways, driven by the wind. They had gotten at least another foot since he pushed off the roofs yesterday. As he leaned against the post at the front of the porch, he began to think of Kate. Now that was a good pastime, daydreaming about some woman he'd just met. He thought the sarcasm might jar him out of it, but no such luck.

He checked on Kate throughout the day, but there wasn't much change, not even in her sleeping position. It was close to 1700, when he opened the door and found the bed empty. He quickly looked round the room and spotted Kate on the window seat, staring out the window. Ravenwood walked up behind her and felt her lean back against him.

"Will it ever stop snowing?" asked Kate.

"Always does eventually," answered Ravenwood. Kate sighed deeply and relaxed against him.

"Are you hungry?" asked Ravenwood.

"Yes." answered Kate, surprise clearly in her voice.

"Don't sound so surprised. It's been nearly 24 hours since you've eaten," explained Ravenwood.

"No wonder I'm hungry. Do we have any food?" Kate asked almost innocently.

"Mister Po always has food," said Ravenwood.

"Thank the Gods. Let's have a shower and go eat," said Kate, heading for the bathroom.

Ravenwood began to chuckle. The woman could be so matter-of-fact. At the same time, she could be so, so, irrational. Maybe irrational wasn't the right word. He would work on it.

She had the shower going, her shirt off, and she was soaping up by the time he joined her. She cheerfully began to soap him as well. That could be a problem, or maybe not. He leaned back against the wall and let her fingers work their magic. It was the best he could do under the circumstances, but once her hip showed improvement, he would need much more.

What did she think about the valley and its inhabitants? They were certainly a colorful group. Kate only added to that color. She gave it a brightness that had been missing. Strange, the difference a day can make. Kate probably thought the same thing.

This place was strangely familiar, not the place, exactly. She had never been to this valley. The people and the situations felt familiar to her, which was absurd because she knew she had never met any of them before. Still, she could not shake the feeling, so she decided to go with it, accept it as normal, and see where it ended. How dangerous could it be?

- She knew Ravenwood was capable of great violence. She could feel it. She also knew he would never intentionally harm her. He might bruise her by accident, but never on purpose, such contradictions in the man.

No, she was in no physical danger. Ravenwood would keep her safe, but if she lost her soul to him, what then? How dangerous could that be?" She just might run if there was not a blizzard dumping snow all over the mountains. Of course, if there had been no blizzard, she would not have ended up here to begin with. It was the old question of the chicken and the egg. Cause and effect and cause again. Round, like a circle in a - Stop that! It would only make her crazy. Stay or go, make a choice and see it through. She had some time to decide, not a lot, but some. Problem was, she felt like she belonged here. It had been a long time since she felt like she belonged somewhere. So long, she had a hard time remembering what it felt like. She could do worse than belong to these people, to this place. She had done worse in the past. Maybe it was time for a change, a good one this time. -

When Ravenwood kept her awake that first night; as they talked, shared, and wondered through the night, their bodies huddled together in the bed keeping warm, the choice was made. In Ravenwood's case, that was not strictly true. He did not have to work to keep warm; he radiated heat like the proverbial stove, which was good, since Kate absorbed it like a sponge. Was this the way it had always been? One warm, one cold, one seeking, the other accepting. Did this keep the human race moving forward, a little matter of heat? They always said opposites attracted, but that was really the only way in which they were opposites. In other ways, they were actually very similar. With that understanding, they got dressed and went down for supper.

Everyone seemed pleased to see her; happy she had waked without any problem. Tonight they had pasta, very good pasta; the sauce was fragrant and sweet. The garlic bread came from a local bakery, but kept well in the freezer. No wonder they had such a large freezer. Food just kept coming out of there. The sauce had come off the shelves. She remembered seeing it in the cabinet. Did Mr. Po also can the food she wondered, so she asked, "Did you can the sauce, Mr. Po? '

"No. Mrs. Harper cans the sauce," said Mr. Po. Kate was confused. This sauce was too good. It had to be from Mr. Po.

The Harpers grow fields of tomatoes. It's their principal crop," explained Jonas. "We buy them by the truckload. Mr. Po turns them into sauce. Mrs. Harper cans the sauce. We have sauce all through the winter."

"You don't grow tomatoes yourselves?" asked Kate.

"No. The Harpers keep us well supplied with fresh tomatoes through the season. Like I said, it's their principal crop," reiterated Jonas.

"I don't know what that means; it's their principal crop," said Kate.

"It means selling it is how they make their money for the year and support their family," said Ravenwood.

"So buying from them supports the local economy and keeps the farmers in business," said Kate.

"Yes. It also makes it not really worth our time to grow tomatoes when somebody else does it for a living and needs the money," said Ravenwood.

"I understand," said Kate.

"You do?" inquired Jamie.

"Yes. It makes sense," said Kate.

"It does?" asked Jamie.

"Of course it does," said Kate.

"We don't raise cows or sheep either," said Jamie.

"Why would we? Our expertise is in raising horses," said Joe.

"So you also buy the steer or lamb locally from the people for whom it is their money crop?" asked Kate, feeling the information roll around in her head.

"Yes," said Ravenwood.

"Just like when they want a horse, they come to us," added Joe.

"Do they need many horses?" inquired Kate.

"The locals, no; the trainers, yes," said Ravenwood.

"Trainers?" questioned Kate.

"Horses go from the breeders – that's us – to the trainers, who actually teach the horse and get them in shape for the season," explained Joe.

"Season?" questioned Kate.

"Racing season," said Joe.

"These are race horses?" asked Kate with surprise.

"Not yet, but many of them will be if we have bred them right," said Joe.

"Every spring the trainers show up to see if anything looks promising. If it does, they make a deal," said Ravenwood.

"Do they usually find something promising?" asked Kate.

"Yes. Bound to learn a thing or two in 40 years," said Joe.

"Know anything about horses or horse racing?" asked Ravenwood.

"Not a thing," said Kate.

"You'll learn the basics soon enough," said Joe.

"Do I need to know the basics?" asked Kate.

"Always easier if everyone involved knows the basics. Saves time on explanations." said Joe.

"After some reflection, Kate asked "Did I do something wrong?"

"No," Joe replied, "nothing wrong."

"That's good. I didn't want to do anything wrong," said Kate cheerfully.

"Doubt you could," replied Ravenwood mysteriously.

"Depends on who defines wrong," said Kate, an odd look passing over her face.

Ravenwood regarded her across the table. Someone had 'defined wrong' very narrowly and strictly, for it to continue to weigh on her mind. He wondered who did the defining.

The chill came over her again. It was always there except when she cuddled with Ravenwood. She needed to exercise her leg. That should warm her up. She struggled from the chair and began her trek to the back of the house. She wondered if there were any exercises to do for her head. They didn't really believe her, that it was broken. She had never met them before yesterday. How would they know if her head was broken or not? She had only found the children yesterday. So much had happened in just one day. Everything was in motion. Nothing was still.

"Mama?" that was not Brynna, that was Gabe.

"Mama, can you bake anything besides cornbread?" asked Gabe. "Your cornbread is really good, but maybe something sweet would be good. Maybe, yes?"

I am willing to try baking just about anything, with one condition," said Kate.

"What is the condition?" asked Gabe.

"You must eat what I bake, even if it's a flop. You can't be refusing to eat it just because it's not perfect. That would be a waste of supplies and just really a bummer," said Kate.

"Disrespectful," supplied Ravenwood.

"What" asked Kate?

"Disrespectful is the word you're looking for. You spend your time and your energy to make something for us and we just walk away because it's not perfect. Disrespectful is the word."

"Yes, thank you. That is the word. How did you know?" asked Kate.

"It's what my mother always said," Ravenwood explained.

"She had the same rule, had my Sara," said Joe. "If I'm going to spend my time and effort making it, you're going to eat it or they'll be no more."

"Oh, I like her," said Kate.

"Aye, you would have. A lot alike, the two of you are," said Joe.

A look of complete doubt took up residence on Kate's face and showed no signs of leaving and she wondered why Joe thought she and Sara were alike.

"Strongest woman I ever knew. Her tongue could peel the skin from your body without leaving a mark," he explained.

"I don't feel very strong," said Kate.

"You been hurt - still are hurt, but you'll heal," said Joe. "It takes a strong woman to ride herd on this clan. Hadn't met anyone I thought could do it since my Sara passed on. Not until yesterday, when you came driving in here."

Disbelief showing clearly on her face, Kate just stared at him.

I know you don't feel it now, but you will and we'll all be the better for it, including you. Wait and see if you're not. Dinna rush off, just wait and see," assured Joe.

Kate got up and began to exercise, and to mutter. "Can't rush anywhere; hip not working; head broken; can't rush anywhere." Even if I could rush, there is a ton of snow out there; drifts 10 feet deep. Snow a couple feet deep even on level ground. What Level ground? There is no level ground here. Mountains were everywhere. Everything goes strait up or straight down or winds around while it does one or the other or," she was working herself into a state. This was not good, not good at all. She needed a few deep breaths and a little vigorous exercise to relieve stress. Vigorous exercise; if she weren't careful, Ravenwood would give her so much vigorous exercise she might never move again. Did she really get him off in the shower earlier? Yes, she did. What exactly was wrong with her? She never did that with someone she just met, and she just met him 2 days ago.

"Did I mention my Sara didn't take any shit from anyone?" asked Joe.

"No, no you didn't. That's good to know," said Kate.

"You're a lot alike, the two of you. Not in your looks, no, but in your ways," said Joe, wandering out to the porch.

"Can I see her picture again?" asked Kate.

Ravenwood went to the Main room and returned with a framed 8x10 wedding picture of his mother and father. Kate was amazed that Joe thought they were similar. Sara Ravenwood had been a full-blooded Cheyenne. She was almost as tall as Joe was, straight and slim as an arrow, with a pride showing through every line of her body. She looked to be an imposing woman, one it was best not to cross. Obviously, her husband and son had loved her deeply. She was not a raving beauty. She was lovely. With her heavy dark hair, her black eyes, and creamy copper skin, she was lovely. That was the word. Moreover, she didn't take any shit from anybody - an intriguing woman.

Perhaps, once the snow cleared, she could visit with Sara and - and commune with the dead? Besides, the snow would not clear until late in the spring. What was she thinking? She was thinking survival. She knew that. What did that mean, exactly? She was in no physical danger. She knew that. She put the picture back in the main Room and began to exercise her hip. It was slow, but she kept moving. This was important, to keep moving, not to allow it to stiffen.

So she moved. Back and forth from the office in the back of the house to the kitchen at the front, until Mr. Po told her that was enough for the day. She looked through the bookshelves in the Main Room, searching for something to read to the children. She found the classics tucked up on a shelf near the top of the bookcase. Fortunately, Luc and Trist were perfectly willing to climb up and get them. She always thought of them together. That was probably unfair. They were separate people with their own personalities. She would have to try harder to separate them in her head. Twain was always a good bet, but she would have to do some prep work on its more racy parts. Dickens did not have such a casual racist tone and it was thick enough to keep them busy for a week. Would it stop snowing in a week? They could only hope. So, 'It was the best of times, it was the worst of times' became the lead story for the evening.

"Gather round and make yourselves comfortable. This is not a children's book, but it is a good story. Its name is A Tale of Two Cities. It is old, so the language is old. Some of the words may no longer be in use or the usage might have changed. If we use some words, you are unfamiliar with or read something you don't understand, just raise your hand and we will stop to discuss it. OK?" They all nodded and so they began. It did not go quickly. There was so much they had questions about, but that was good wasn't it. When they questioned, they learned. By the time she was ready to end the session, she realized that the room was full and everyone was fascinated. Joe, Gully, Charlie, Jonas, Jamie, Mr. Po, Ravenwood; they were all settled round the perimeter of the room, rapt in the story. By the time she ended the session, she was exhausted, but she promised to read again the next night so the children did not grumble – much.

Kate headed to the kitchen for a snack. "Mister Po, do we have the ingredients to make cookies?" she asked.

"What kind of cookies?" Mister Po responded.

"Chocolate chip, I think," said Kate. No one has any food allergies I should know about, do they."

"No allergies. Some things they like better than others, but no allergies," Mister Po assured her.

"I thought I could try the cookies tomorrow after breakfast, if that's all right with you," said Kate.

"That would be fine, Kate. The children will be thrilled," said Mr. Po.

All the other men had gone outside for a cigar.

"You don't smoke, do you, Mr. Po?" asked Kate.

"Rarely," replied Mister Po, "Never really cared for it. Got the habit during the war, but it was easily broken."

"That's good. Good for you," said Kate quietly.

"Don't you think you need more sleep?" asked Mister Po.

"I slept for almost a whole day," said Kate. "Shouldn't that be enough for a few hours?"

"Yes, you slept for a whole day, but you had been sleep deprived for the entire day before. And the scales don't balance that evenly," explained Mr. Po.

"Is that the polite way of saying – Go to Bed?" asked Kate.

"Yes," said Mr. Po, laughing softly.

"OK," said Kate, starting for the stairs.

"Kate, stairs are not good yet," cautioned Mister Po. "Better to be carried for now."

Jamie obediently carried her to the top of the stairs, depositing her gently there to make her way to the bedroom. By the time she arrived, she was very tired, and barely took time to remove her shoes and pull up the blanket before crawling into bed and falling asleep. How odd that she needed more sleep so quickly she thought - and then she was gone.

When Ravenwood came to bed some time later, he found her curled on her right side, nothing showing but the top of her head peaking out of the quilts. He soon discovered that she was still fully dressed under the quilts. She hadn't even taken the time to remove her bra. Now that had to be uncomfortable. He never had understood under wires. How women could wear them was a mystery, but Kate said the others just didn't have enough support. That was his total knowledge on the subject so he just removed it and continued. In fact, he removed all her clothes. She never woke up and she went easily into his arms, seeking warmth and comfort. He wrapped her close, holding her tightly against him, and thought of tomorrow, of all their tomorrows.

Kate woke with a twitch. She did that sometimes. She didn't know why. She knew that it woke Ravenwood, but he gave no sign of it other than to squeeze her tighter against him - too tight, much too tight.

"Not breathing - too tight," she said, tapping her fist against his chest. He immediately loosened his hold on her. He didn't realize how strong he way – and how fragile she could be. He would pay more attention in the future. He had learned years ago to be very careful around the children. He could hurt them without intention, without much thought at all. It was the same with Kate. He knew that wasn't entirely true, but it helped get his head in the right place so he did not accidentally hurt her. Whether it was literally true was beside the point. He needed to make her safe, even from himself.

"Are you all right, Ravenwood," asked Kate.

"Yes, are you," replied Ravenwood.

"Of course," said Kate.

"Are you sure," questioned Ravenwood.

Kate levered up on her elbow and put her face very close to his.

"What are you afraid of?" she asked.

"Hurting you: thoughtlessly, carelessly, casually," he replied.

"I understand you are very strong. I understand you trained in the brutality of war. I understand you learned discipline and control to survive. I am not afraid of you, Ravenwood," Kate said softly, but firmly. "Please do not be afraid of me."

Ravenwood looked at her as if she had lost her mind. Then, when he thought about it, he knew she was right. He couldn't let his fear of hurting her keep him from his life that could be. So OK - he would be mindful and she would not be fearful. They would live without hesitation and debate. He wondered how long they would have together. As always, it would be long enough - too much reflection this morning, too much. He tossed back the covers and got out of bed just as the hall door opened.

Jonas stepped into the bedroom, saying, "I think we have a problem. Bobby Miller has disappeared. I've looked all over the house."

"Everyone is somewhere, Jonas. No one just disappears in a puff of smoke," explained Kate.

"Uh huh," said Jonas sounding skeptically. Kate was surprised he hadn't made their traditional sound of disgust and disbelief.

"She is right," said Ravenwood, pulling on clothes as he spoke. Sounds simple enough, but rarely is."

Kate sat up, forgetting that she was completely naked, or maybe she didn't realize it. After all, she was asleep. Ravenwood was the one who undressed her. As the quilt fell to her waist, she grabbed for it and hugged it back into place, her blush a lovely shade of rosy pink had Jonas and Ravenwood both grinning mindlessly as they stared.

"Don't we have a missing child," asked Kate. "Shouldn't you be looking for him," she got no response to either question and in exasperation with them both she ordered," Go find Bobby Miller."

They obediently left the room, but stopped moving as soon as the door closed. Ravenwood shook his head to clear it. Jonas stood staring at the wall in front of him, the blank wall. Damn, her tits were sweet. Full and heavy; they would fill a man's hand generously, even his hand, especially his hand.

"Have you already given the dogs the scent and let them outside?" asked Ravenwood.

"Yes. They didn't hit on anything, not on the porch or further out in the yard," answered Jonas.

"We should concentrate on the inside of the house. When did you last see him," asked Ravenwood.

"It was around 0300 this morning; I was checking the fires upstairs and made a pass through the ground floor just to make sure everything was OK. Bobby had kicked his blankets back and curled up against the cold. I pulled them back up and tucked them around him. Then I went back to bed," explained Jonas.

"Where was he sleeping," asked Ravenwood. It was only around 0600 now and the rest of the children were sprawled over the floor. There were no extra blankets. Wherever Bobby had gone, the blankets were gone with him.

"He was here, furthest from the fire," said Jonas. Ravenwood sank down on his haunches and looked at the floor carefully. It was hardwood with scattered rugs. He rose quickly from his contemplation of the floor, and walked to the closet off to the side of the fireplace. As he opened the door he said, "You can come out now, Bobby. Nothing will happen to you."

At first, they heard nothing, but then there was a small scraping noise followed by a clunk and then there was Bobby: small, frail, and obviously frightened. By now, Kate had dressed and scooted down the stairs. She was now quite good at scooting. As she came thumping slowly into the Living Room, Bobby threw himself into her arms. Both of them would have gone down if Ravenwood had not caught them, or more precisely, her. He didn't' really care if Bobby went down, but Bobby did not go down. He fastened to Kate like a leach and stuck tight, crying soundlessly. That was the spooky part, the soundless crying.

Kate sat and rocked him, trying to comfort him. They removed to the kitchen so they would not wake the other children, and still he cried. Something had happened. He was fine last night. Now he cried and cringed every time one of the men came near him. As they set about making coffee and tea and normal morning stuff, Kate watched Bobby closely. He sat squirming on the chair next to her - Squirming from side to side, half standing, and then sitting back, only to change position again.

"Oh, my God!" said Kate and then said no more. She shoo'd the men out of the kitchen so she could talk to Bobby. She hardly knew what to say, what to ask. If what she suspected was true, he would not want to talk about it, but she could not leave him to suffer.

"Bobby has someone been hurting you and threatened you into silence if you try to tell anyone?" asked Kate.

Bobby just looked at the floor and said nothing. Then very slowly, he nodded his head. The story came out in starts and stops. It took a long time, but rushing was not an option.

His father visited his bed at night several times a week: Always at night, always in secret, always threatening him with more pain if he told. The child could barely sit as it was. Some days he could not sit long enough to attend class so he just walked down to the creek and soaked his bum in the cold water. When Jonas had tucked the blankets back around him last night, it had triggered his fear; he needed a small space to feel safe, so he went for the closet, taking his blanket and pillow with him. No one could sneak up on him there.

Kate explained that no man here would hurt him: no man, not Ravenwood, not Jonas, not Mr. Po, Gully, or Charlie, no one. He could sleep in the closet if he wanted, but no one would hurt him here. The other children, having been fed and sent out to play on the porch, could not hear Bobby's story. It took some convincing, but he finally agreed to let Mr. Po check his bum if Kate stayed in the room with him as Mr. Po did his exam. He made it quick and as painless as possible. Then he gave him some crème and explained how and when to use it, applying the first treatment himself so Bobby would understand how much it would help, and it did help.

As the other children came back into the house, they began to tease him about not being outside with them, about being teacher's pet, about being a mama's boy. Kate knew that trying to stop it would only make it worse so she said nothing. Joe pulled Bobby aside and had a few words with him and the next time they teased him about being teacher's pet, he just grinned and said nothing. They teased him about being a mama's boy, but he just grinned and said nothing. Eventually, they stopped teasing him, especially when he didn't ask for anything special.

Bobby continued to use the crème on his bum whenever it felt tight, dry, or itched unbearably and he continued to improve. In addition, it continued to snow. It had been a full week now, with the blizzard raging outside. Kate began to take her exercise on the porch. Since the porch went all the way around the house and the breezeway through the center, it was convenient for doing laps, and that is what she did.

It started with half a lap. Once that became easier, she increased the distance a little. Do not push too fast. Slow and steady will show the most improvement. Every morning the snow had drifted up around the house, covering portions of the porch. Ravenwood solved that problem by having the boys shovel off the porch every morning, with the rest of the children taking turns throughout the day. He worried about ice and would check the porch periodically. He knew if her cane hit a patch of ice she would go down and maybe this time something would be broken, something besides her head.

Sometimes the wind threatened to blow her over, but she kept moving. The resistance made her stronger. That was the way of things. There was a famous quote about that; which she couldn't remember right now, but she was sure would come to her later.

At first, the snowflakes were huge and fluffy, then they were small and piercing, like ice pellets screaming against her skin. She wrapped up from head to foot, with an extra scarf over her face. It was amazing she could see at all, but she didn't have to see much to get around the porch. By the time she headed back inside, she was cold, tired, and thoroughly irritated at herself. She was so slow and awkward. Would she be like this forever? What a depressing thought. Mr. Po said she was healing nicely and would continue to grow stronger.

Hmgph was her response – and then she would laugh delightedly. That was such a satisfying sound, somewhere between a snort of disbelief and a snarl of disgust; it made her feel better almost immediately - wonderful sound!

The snow eventually stopped, as Ravenwood had predicted so long ago. The roads were eventually passable, if not completely cleared. The Ravenwoods took care of their own driveway up until it connected with the state highway. Driveway was such an innocuous word for that stretch of road. After it left the highway, it cut straight through the mountain in a tunnel about 15 feet high and 20 feet wide. The family called it the gate.

After it passed through the gate, it was still several miles across the valley to the main house. It was hard to tell distance when everything was covered in white fluff and she was never very good at it anyway.

With the clearing of the roads came the families to pick up their children. The Ravenwoods managed to get a message to the sheriff before the storm hit full strength and he notified the families, not only that their children were safe, and where they could be picked up after the storm, but how they had been rescued and by whom. Her name was Kate. She was a stranger to the valley. They would love her forever for saving their children. They immediately thought of her as Miss Kate.

When a car passed through the gate, a buzzer sounded on the monitoring unit located off the kitchen. They knew who was coming since there were cameras mounted in the tunnel. It was a simple and effective little security system. Kate was doing her rounds on the porch when the first cars arrived and the first children flew out the front and into their parent's arms.

"Mama Kate, Mama Kate, these are my parents," cried Sheryl excitedly.

"It's very nice to meet you," said Kate politely.

"It's a pleasure to meet you, Miss Kate, a real pleasure," said Sheryl's father, shaking her hand. Her mother just threw her arms around Kate and cried. Kate began to panic. The woman had her over balanced. Fortunately, Ravenwood appeared behind her to steady her and uncoil the woman from around her. No easy task, that, since the mother was now sobbing noisily and clutching Kate tightly. Boa constrictors came to mind. Kate knew that was unkind, but she couldn't help it. Ravenwood finally got her detached and her husband helped her down from the porch. "Miss Kate, we do thank you. If ever you need anything..." His voice trailed off as he looked back and forth between Kate and Ravenwood.

He looked directly into Ravenwood's eyes, "If she needs, you call." Ravenwood nodded in acknowledgement of the message. Sheryl hugged Kate and said goodbye and the little group moved down to the car and got in.

This scene repeated many times over the next few days as families reunited, children jumping for joy, expressing their thanks, saying goodbye. It was exhausting for Kate. They always asked for her if she was not already out on the porch. They always hugged her, at least the women did. The men were more reserved and settled for a handshake, especially once Ravenwood appeared behind her. He really had the most spectacular glare. Much seemed to be communicated with a nod and a handshake. Kate found it very confusing. Soon all the children were gone except Bobby. He certainly wasn't complaining. He had been growing happier by the day. He no longer had to use the crème. He no longer had pain.

Then one day Robin Miller showed up. Everyone was gone from the house except Kate and the children. Luc immediately rang the bell that called his father.

"Come on Bobby. You been here long enough," said Mr. Miller. Bobby was hiding behind Kate and did not move.

"What lies have you been telling these people? This woman saved your life. Don't you think she deserves the truth?" agued Mr. Miller.

"They got a restraining order against me. I'm not supposed to come within 100 feet of you: no touching, no hugging, and no communication at all. What's that all about, Bobby? What lies have you told them?" yelled Mr. Miller. He was truly angry now and he got louder as he came up the steps to the porch. Luc and Trist positioned themselves at the top of the stairs between Mr. Miller and Kate.

"You come out from behind her Bobby. You come out and talk to me like a man and we'll settle this," yelled Mr. Miller.

Something snapped inside Bobby, "Talk to you like a man?" he asked incredulously.

"You been raping me for months you butt fucking son-on-a-bitch. Where do you get off telling me to talk to you like a man? You're not a man. You're certainly not a father and I don't want you anywhere near me. You get in your car and get the hell away from me," screamed Bobby, his anger bubbling over at last.

He launched himself from the top step and landed on his father's chest, knocking him to the ground. Luc and Trist, deciding this was a grand idea, promptly penned his arms while Bobby jumped up and down on his chest and other parts more relevant to the problem. Bobby was practically doing a war dance on top of his father while Luc and Trist provided the music. Kate was so astonished that her mouth fell open and no sound came out. For one of the few times in her life, she was speechless. Mr. Miller had no such problem. He was now howling in pain and anger.

As Ravenwood strode into the yard, he looked at his sons and said, "Enough." They immediately stopped their chanting and moved away. Ravenwood plucked Bobby off the top of his father and tossed him in the general direction of the boys so they all went down in a tangle. Finally, he looked at Miller, who was almost his height and about 30 pounds heavier and said, "Leave, now."

"I am not leaving without my son," said Miller loudly.

"I can always arrange for you not to leave at all, if that's your preference," said Ravenwood mildly.

"No, that is not my preference and don't you threaten me. I don't care who you are. You have no right to keep me from my son," yelled Mr. Miller, the words in total free fall from his mouth.

"What about Bobby's rights, "asked Ravenwood as he moved closer to Miller, his demeanor clearly threatening.

"Be gone now," said Ravenwood, his voice low, his body ready. Why not, he thought. It would reduce some of the tension he had felt since Kate's arrival. He had a primeval need to beat someone, who, did not really matter. Miller would do nicely. Besides, he was a pedophile. He had already scarred Bobby's life. It would take years to recover what he had stolen, if that was even possible.

Mr. Miller decided to follow instructions and be gone. "You'll hear from me again, Ravenwood. Don't think you won't," yelled Miller.

"Hmgph," was Ravenwood's only response. He looked down at the three snow covered urchins who danced around him. How could he be angry with them for doing what he had wanted to do himself? It was something about the chanting and the stomping that had spooked Kate. She was not easily scared, but she could be spooked. It was an eerie scene, with the children chanting and Bobby dancing on top of his father. It reminded her of some book she had been required to read at school.

"Da, what's a butt fucking SOB?" whispered Brynna seriously.

"Where did you hear that expression?" asked Ravenwood.

"It's what Bobby called his father just before he jumped him," answered Kate.

"Thank you for that," said Ravenwood.

"You're welcome," replied Kate, not without some humor.

Brynna, Gabe, and Sela were all following this conversation between Ravenwood and Kate closely. It was like a tennis match.

"Brynna, its not an expression children should use. Your mother will explain why after lunch," said Ravenwood, sending the first volley.

"Thank you for that," from Kate.

"You're welcome," replied Ravenwood, heading for the front door.

"Mama, why do we have to wait until after lunch," asked Gabe.

"I suppose he was just giving me time to think of how to explain it," said Kate.

"I can explain it," offered Bobby loudly.

"Pipe down," ordered Kate briskly, which he did. Now all the children stood silently looking at her, waiting for an explanation. Oh, she would make him suffer, thought Kate.

She explained without euphemism, bluntly and straight to the point. Ravenwood usually supplied this explanation: nothing was sugar coated, nothing concealed. A little graphic maybe, but at least they knew where the dangers were. When she finished reassuring them and left them to discuss it among themselves, she walked into the house to find Ravenwood listening just inside the front door.

"Well done for your first time, Kate," he greeted her.

"You could have picked something easier," she replied.

"It was the first thing that came up," he explained.

"Oh, very funny," Kate said sarcastically. "You'll pay for this one, Ravenwood."

"Everyone has to start somewhere. Any idea how much it's going to cost?"

"No. Calculating these rates is new to me."

"Maybe we should go upstairs and negotiate," offered Ravenwood.

"Maybe you should come to lunch and think about it," said Mr. Po from the kitchen doorway.

Ravenwood gave him a look that clearly told him to drop dead. Mr. Po shrugged it off and called everyone in for lunch.

The children were still chattering about the subject, until Kate reminded them it was not good table conversation. Once the children had finished eating and left the table, Joe looked at Ravenwood and Kate and asked very directly, "What, exactly, did we miss this morning?"

Ravenwood filled him in, with Kate adding bits and pieces as they went, especially when it got to the part of who would answer Brynna's question. Joe just agreed with Ravenwood – She had to start somewhere. He also agreed with Kate. Da was going to pay for that one, deservedly so.

The next day the schools were officially open again and all the children except Brynna left early. It was eerie, getting back on a school bus, but it needed doing. Besides, the more they delayed, the larger it would get. Therefore, they all went back to school, including Bobby. It was a good idea, useful if they decided to prosecute his father. It might even force him out of the state. It would be hard on the little boy, which was why Jonas hesitated to file charges.

While they waited to see if Bobby was strong enough for a trial, Ravenwood took Kate in to see Dr. Raab. He had been a doctor at the town clinic for 30 years. Before that, he had a little office on the edge of town where people came and waited to see him – first come, first served. Dr. Raab did not have a specialty, but he had seen more of just about any kind of illness or injury that anyone in the state. He and Mr. Po had a mutual respect for each other and often collaborated on diagnosis and treatment. It didn't matter to Dr. Raab that Mr. Po had no license to practice medicine in the U.S. It wasn't as if Mr. Po was going to work at the clinic and treat people for payment. He just helped where he could. As Ravenwood waited outside the clinic, Dr. Raab and Mr. Po discussed Kate and her broken head. The hip was healing nicely. The bruise had gone to a bluish green and if she kept moving would continue to improve. Nothing was broken. Her head was another matter.

Dr. Raab gave her a few verbal tests. The results were unclear. Some of her answers were just strange. What was that expression - nonsequitur? Kate's answers did not seem to relate directly to the questions asked. He ordered some tests to see what they could see. He wanted to keep her for a few days observation, but she wasn't having any of that and Ravenwood backed her up. They made an odd pair. It would be interesting to watch their relationship develop. He had to assume there was a relationship because Mr. Po said nothing and nobody kept a secret better than Ravenwood when he wanted to.

They made an appointment to hear test results the following week and then visited the Moonlight Emporium. It was a large and fascinating place. Merchandise stretched for blocks with massive variety. There were spices, jewelry, furniture, and paintings and - it was how she imagined a bazaar in the east, perhaps Casablanca or Morocco or Marrakech. A woman named Stella ran it. She was a slim, energetic brunette aged somewhere around 60. She knew every category of merchandise she carried. One of those categories was furniture and one of the lines of furniture was Salt and Gull. They had their own special display section near the center of the emporium. Stella complained that sales were much faster than restocking.

They just told her that quality work takes time and she had to be content with that.

As Ravenwood discussed terms with Stella, Kate wandered the aisles. Some things here were very rare. Some things were obscure or hard to find, but were not expensive once found. She saw a sign that read, 'Original Home of Po's Potions'. Po's Potions, - what were Po's Potions? They were one cleanser and one moisturizer. They worked on all skin types. They worked on the hair as well as the skin. Production only happened once a year and they had a fixed run size. Stella found her staring at the display and began to brag on the potions.

"How old do you think I am," asked Stella openly.

"I have no idea," replied Kate.

Stella laughed delightedly, "All right, I'm 65 next month. I've been using Po's Potions for the past three years. Every year I look younger. Most people in town use it with the same results. Hell, women all over the country swear by it and try to stock up every season when it comes on the market," explained Stella.

"How long does a bottle last," asked Kate?

"It will last a good year, longer if you're careful, not as long if you share," said Stella with speculation in her eyes. Kate just smiled and kept moving.

"You know Ravenwood has been chased by nearly every woman in the state at one time or another. So has Jonas, and Joe, and they been chasing Jamie since he could walk," said Stella.

"Why," asked Kate?

"Oh, there is just something about those Ravenwood boys," said Stella. "They live up there in the valley. They support themselves with their own businesses. They only come to town when there is something they need and, damn, they are gorgeous to look at. Hell on wheels when they get rolling, but gorgeous to look at."

With that, Stella went off to help a customer, leaving a bemused Kate to wander the store. She wondered where Mr. Po and Ravenwood had gone, but soon discovered them at one of the back loading docks.

Charlie and Gully had brought some furniture in to sell. Everyone helped unload the truck and move the furniture into position in the show room. As she watched them work, Kate acknowledged that Stella was correct – There was just something about those Ravenwood boys. There obviously had been for many generations and would be for several more. Interesting, how women were drawn to them, and how they behaved when around. Kate dropped into the middle of the clan and Ravenwood claimed her. Oh, he offered to let her choose another, but she understood now that he was only being polite in a strange way. If she had chosen another 'bed', there would have been hell all over the valley and far beyond. They were not yet lovers, but she belonged to him in a way that was new to her. It felt like a merging of sorts and it moved deep within her – so powerful – so wondrous. It defied description. It needed none; no description, no explanation, no justification, it just was. Ravenwood seemed to understand it in the same fashion as well. There had been no deep discussions of love and philosophy and goals and dreams. It was all decided that first night and did not need revisiting. She felt amazingly comfortable with the arrangement. She had been in control all her life. Now she was content to have Ravenwood take care of her. It would not do for anyone else to try. She knew that. She had never felt so free. She found a chair and sat down to wait until the furniture staging and pricing was complete.

Stella soon joined her and began a conversation. For a family tucked away in the mountains, they had a lot of influence on the community. The Ravenwoods could not be bought, bullied, or beaten. They spent their money locally and they helped directly, not by contributing money to some fund, but by working your fields if you got hurt or driving your produce to market. Bottom line was, they had the respect of the town and the surrounding farmers and their opinion carried weight. It was somewhat amazing, since it was clear that the Ravenwood's did not much care what anyone thought about them or what they did.

"Ms. Ravenwood! Ms. Ravenwood!" said a strange voice. Evidently, Kate had drifted off and someone wanted her attention.

"Ms. Ravenwood, my editor really wants an interview for the Sunday paper. I really need to speak with you," said the voice urgently.

"Now, Kyle, you know she ain't Ms. Ravenwood. Why don't you call her Miss Kate, like everyone else in town," said Stella?

Kate opened her eyes and regarded a slender young man with short-cropped red curls and deep brown eyes who looked so very earnest that he made you want to help him. That was his hook.

"Miss Kate, my name is Kyle Borden. It's a real pleasure to meet you," said Kyle, holding out his hand in greeting.

Kate looked at Kyle. She looked at the extended hand and tilted her head slightly sideways in what she thought of as her confused puppy dog look. Taking the proffered hand, she asked, "Why?"

"Why what, Ma'am?" asked Kyle.

"Why is it a real pleasure to meet me?" Kate asked.

"Well ma'am, you just saved the lives of the children of some of the most prominent members of this community. The whole town is grateful, "explained Kyle.

Some of its most prominent members and one butt fucking SOB she thought. She wondered if the prominent community members knew what Mr. Miller did every night. She thought not. These were direct people, and they wouldn't have time for any thing so filthy or so hurtful to a child.

"Please be gone, Mr. Borden," said Kate politely, but firmly.

"Ma'am?" questioned Kyle in surprise.

Stella laughed and then clarified, "That's a real polite way of telling you to hit the road, take a hike, leave her alone, and get lost. Clear it up any?"

"But ma'am, I just need to get this interview. It won't take long. My editor needs a story on how you found those kids and I need to…"

"I was lost," said Kate, "completely and totally lost. It was pure chance." Then she walked away, actually she lurched away, since her limp was still very pronounced.

Kyle stared after her in amazement. He started after her only to find his way blocked completely by Ravenwood. "Mr. Ravenwood," Kyle squeaked," I was just asking Miss Kate some questions about the day she found the children. She says she was completely lost. Is that right?"

Ravenwood just shrugged one shoulder and kept moving. These people were very frustrating. How was he supposed to get an answer to anything?

"Son, you best move your butt before somebody runs over it," said Stella with a smile. Kyle turned to see a large chest headed directly for him. He jumped into a side aisle and watched as two men brought the chest to a stop and deftly swing it into position on the showroom floor. He wondered where Miss Kate had gone. He needed a better story than – I was lost. I was completely and totally lost. - Or maybe he didn't. Could he sell that to his editor? Was there an angle here that he had not seen? If she was so lost, then who or what had guided her to the bus - Devine providence - The hand of god. A big grin broke out across his face. People loved that shit. He could work this for weeks.

"How often do we restock the furniture," asked Kate on the way home.

"It depends on the season. It sells steadily all year round, but summer is the market. That's when there is the most traffic through the Emporium," explained Charlie.

"Do you sell from anywhere else," asked Kate.

"No. It's too much trouble. We just take it to Stella and she does the rest, the same as Mr. Po," said Gully. Kate was in the truck with Charlie and Gully. Ravenwood had said he needed to run an errand and that she should go home on the truck. He would join her shortly. Now what was that all about? It didn't really matter. He would tell her when they got home.

When they got home – What an interesting phrase that was. It had not really had any significance for her in quite some time – now it did.

Kate sat quietly between the two men, her thoughts rambling everywhere. Could any of those tests of Dr. Raab show the chaos of thought? She suddenly looked over at the farmhouse they were passing and shuddered slightly.

"What's wrong," asked Gully.

"That's a bad place," replied Kate.

Charlie and Gully looked at each other over her head and just shrugged. One day they would understand, but today was not that day.

Ravenwood was already home when they got there so whatever he had gone to do had not taken long. When he came out of the house to greet them, the smile that moved over Kate's face was wondrous to behold. Her whole body radiated happiness. As Ravenwood wrapped his arms around her, so did his. It was kind of like a cocoon that surrounded them both. Charlie wondered how long that would last. Ravenwood's record with women was atrocious. Women adored him, they chased him, they showed him a good time and then they left. He always could get women, but they just never stayed.

After they had collected the kids, and brought them to the valley, Sara told him he needed to get them a mother. He had not taken it too seriously until after Sara died. That's when the real rush started. He, and the children, soon tired of the games. It had gotten so bad; the children could spot them as soon as they stepped out of their car. The Ravenwoods installed a simple warning system in the gate, with a remote control for convenience. It was a pain in the ass, just to keep some women under control. Of course, it didn't just help Ravenwood. There was Joe, Jonas, and Jamie to think of, and Luc and Trist were growing fast. As Stella said, "There's just something about those Ravenwood boys."

These Ravenwood boys were not complaining, not really. They might fuss sometimes, but there was no real complaint. They enjoyed women. They enjoyed every woman who came their way. Regardless of size, shape, or color, they enjoyed them all. The women just circled around the family unit. They never entered it when they arrived; they left no holes when they departed. Kate was the exception. She immediately entered the family unit. Not only did she enter it, she took center stage, and she wasn't even trying. Opinions outside the valley did not really matter to the Ravenwoods and they didn't care how jealous other women were of Kate. It was a thing to which she would adjust. She might find it strange at first, but she would adjust. Sara had found it strange her whole life, the strange jealousies of other people.

Perhaps Kate would find it easier, or not. It was what it was, as Joe would say.

One Wedding

Currently, life was wonderful. All the inhabitants of the valley circled round Kate and Ravenwood. They were the power, different as they were, and when they combined, they were formidable. You had only to see them together to recognize it. It would only intensify when they actually became lovers, which could not happen soon enough to suit Ravenwood.

He knew he was much too heavy for her hip to withstand the weight. He also knew she was working hard, but it was taking a while to recover. He tried to be patient. He thought they could work it out if she was on top. He wondered how she felt about that. Tonight might be the night to find out. Sounded like a fine idea. They had already established that neither of them had any diseases, he could not get her pregnant, and she was past the age of having children. You could cover a lot of ground talking through a long night. Therefore, if she liked to ride, there was nothing stopping them.

After dinner, Kate read aloud as usual. When the younger children were in bed and the older children were finishing their homework, she and Ravenwood drifted into their bedroom, where he began his slow assault on her senses.

Oh, they had a fine time, just fine. Kate had never thought of herself as a particularly sensuous person, not before the rape and certainly not after. Now she realized that she had never allowed herself to be sensual. There was too much danger there. She had to be careful what kind of man she attracted. She had to be in control all the time. She was vulnerable. She had to be careful. All that mantra went straight out the window. She gave over control. She felt powerful. She was with the quintessential bad boy. She had never felt so safe, so secure. Nothing that gave pleasure to them both was off limits. He encouraged her to explore and she returned the favor.

When she finally sat astride him, slowly sinking onto his cock, he thought he had died and gone to heaven. How did any woman her age get so incredibly tight? He was afraid he might hurt her. He should slow down until her body had a chance to adjust. She suddenly leaned forward, slid her arms around him, and pulled herself snugly against his body. She let out a gasp that was also part moan, and then went very still.

"Breathe, Kate. You must breathe," said Ravenwood. She did breathe - slowly. He watched her chest rise and fall from a particularly wonderful vantage point. Now his hands taught her hips the movement he so badly needed. As she rode him intently, her head tilted back, her eyes half closed, that same moaning/gasping sound combination came from her lips. When she leaned back and circled her hips, her whole body suddenly convulsed. The ripples moving through her belly stroked his cock and made him arch beneath her. He wanted her to have as much pleasure as possible and he tried to hold on, but it was so intense – the sensations she sent through him grabbed him by the balls and squeezed. That expression – it felt so good that it hurt – now he understood what it meant. When he joined her in climax, it exhausted them both. She collapsed on his chest. He did not move, could not move. They lay that way for a while. There was no need to hurry now. They just indulged in the pleasure of each other.

"Are you all right, Kate?" Ravenwood whispered after a time.

"Much more than all right," Kate whispered back, "much more," and she was.

As his breathing returned to normal and the tremors slowed in her body, Kate looked up at her lover and stroked her knuckles over the scar that streaked across his cheekbone.

"Beloved Warrior," she said quietly.

"Golden Cat," he replied just as quietly.

"It took a long time to find me this time," she observed.

"I'd almost given up this time," said Ravenwood.

"That would truly be a shame, not to find you in this life; to die without smelling the wood smoke and the fir trees from our first mating. That would truly be such a shame," said Kate. Ravenwood knew from the time he could walk that he needed to find this woman to be complete. He did not know her name. He did not know what she looked like. He did not know where she was. The need to find her drove him on. This time it had driven him around the world. That was not a first. He had been round the world in many previous lives, but he usually found her first. It was of no importance. They had years and years to live together and grow old, very old.

When they weren't down for breakfast, the men just looked at each other and said Ravenwood must have found a way.

When they weren't down for lunch, they began to worry about exactly what had happened and if it was still happening. Joe caught Brynna standing outside the door with her hand raised and an intent look on her face. She wanted her mama. She wanted her now. Joe did his best to explain, but Brynna was only three after all. It was good they were lovers. He knew it would be good.

They joined the family for dinner. There were no explanations and no questions and no comments – except when Ravenwood suddenly walked back into the Living room, grabbed a pillow, and placed it on the seat of Kate's chair. Then she sat down, gingerly. Gabe asked if she was hurt. She told him no, but that sometimes the chairs were just too hard and wasn't it nice that his father made sure she had a lovely pillow. The children looked skeptical, but didn't say anything more. After they finished eating and left the table, Joe looked at Ravenwood and commented,

"You caught onto that a lot quicker than I did. Your mother had to explain it to me rather graphically before I understood."

"It's not a thing a man would necessarily understand without some explanation," said Ravenwood. Jamie just looked confused and Jonas smiled and whispered a few words in his ear, which cleared the confusion from his face. That sent a blush creeping up Kate's neck. She really was not used to this sort of thing. Joe's comment that Ravenwood 'always had been hung like a horse' only caused the blush to take up permanent radiance on her cheeks.

"Like that should be any surprise, given that you've already said Mom had the same problem," retorted Ravenwood.

"How long does it last, do you think," asked Jamie?

"Hopefully, not long," replied Ravenwood. Kate sat up straighter and glared at them all.

"I like my pillow. I think I will just keep it," she said succinctly. No one argued with her. The pillow was hers as long as she wanted it. In fact, anything she wanted was hers, but all she wanted right now was her pillow.

The men drifted out to the porch for a cigar. The children finished homework and began to gather in the Living room. They wanted to hear the next chapter of the book. The moon was nearly full tonight. As Ravenwood turned from the gleam of moonlight on fresh snow, he saw through the front window a startling tableau. Kate sat in the chair by the fire, Brynna tucked against her side. The other children were scattered on the floor, draped on the furniture, and generally curved and curled into any position that was comfortable.

This was excessively Norman Rockwell for him. He had always been on the edge, always testing the boundaries of what was acceptable. His woman sat reading to his children in the glow of firelight. Their eager faces turned to Kate, who practically radiated light from within. How long had it been since he had seen anything so peaceful? It had been a long time – a damn long time.

Life in the valley was generally peaceful. They didn't go in for much drama there, but this scene was special and he knew it. He was seeing the picture of what the rest of his life could be like. All he had to do was, not screw up.

"Let's walk, son," said Joe beside him.

Ravenwood looked out over the ground, seeing snowdrifts and struggle in his near future, but Joe just set off around the porch. They walked and smoked in silence for a time until Joe said quietly," You know it's important that she stay?"

"Yes," responded Ravenwood.

"You know that you're the only one who can make her want to stay," said Joe.

"Working on it, "responded Ravenwood.

"You do actually talk to her don't you? I mean, I've heard you laugh several times since she's been here so I'm thinking that the two of you do communicate, but I just wanted to make sure. Kate communicates all the time. Be a shame if somebody was not returning her signals. She just might get frustrated and leave," opined Joe. This being one of the longer speeches Ravenwood had ever heard from him, and the subject being communication, it all struck him as funny and he began to laugh. Once started, he could not stop. Shortly, Ravenwood was howling with laughter and holding onto the porch rail for support.

They drew a crowd. The children appeared at the windows. The rest of the men peaked around the corner of the house. "That's pretty encouraging, don't you think," asked Jonas.

"Damn spooky is what it is," said Charlie without hesitation.

The side door to the house opened and Kate appeared on the porch. Stopping directly in front of the two men she said," Papa Joe, what are you doing to Ravenwood?" This question sent Ravenwood into another gale of laughter and made Joe look around him for some sort of support.

"He's behaving strangely, so you must be doing something," Kate insisted. With this statement, she stepped between the two men, facing Joe, her back to Ravenwood. Joe would swear she was prepared to defend him against attack, but Ravenwood needed about as much defending as a mountain lion in a room full of town cats. Still, she had her hands on her hips and a gleam in her eye. Joe considered both omens of bad things to come.

Ravenwood had his laughter somewhat under control and he slid his arms around her waist from behind and pulled her close, burying his face in her hair, chuckling into her ear. Kate reached up to curve her hand round the back of his neck, sliding it under his braid, looking up into his eyes. Ravenwood slid his cheek against hers and she rocked him gently.

"Joe was just checking to make sure I was actually talking to you," said Ravenwood.

Kate tilted her head and looked suspiciously at him. Then she turned and looked suspiciously at Joe," Don't be glaring at me, Sis," Joe said, backing away down the porch. He kept on moving even after he reached the corner and disappeared from sight.

"Ravenwood, your father is behaving strangely," observed Kate.

"Yes he is," agreed Ravenwood.

"Any special reason for it?" asked Kate.

"Just you, honey, just you," answered Ravenwood.

"You do know that you are making no sense, don't you," Kate asked seriously.

"Yes, I do," agreed Ravenwood.

"OK, but I really hope it doesn't become a habit with the two of you," said Kate as she began to lead him back to the front of the house.

"No, ma'am," said Ravenwood. "I'll try to control it."

"That would be a good thing. A person really doesn't need this kind of Sturm und Drang all the time."

"Yes, ma'am, I understand," agreed Ravenwood.

He couldn't remember exactly what Sturm und Drang was, but he did have a general understanding of what she was saying and that was enough for now.

Ravenwood thought wryly on how strange it was that Kate should explain to him that their lives had too much drama in them. It had been a roller coaster ride since she came through the gate in the middle of a blizzard. It would probably continue that way for the rest of their lives. There could be peace and quiet without her versus Sturm und Drang with her. Not even a close choice. He would learn to mitigate the fallout, keep any damages to a minimum, and they would live long happy lives, with the occasional glitch for drama. He should be used to it by now. After 300 years, a man gets used to many things.

Who was crying? He could hear it clearly. It came from outside the house. Their face would freeze if they stayed out here long like that. He eventually found Bobby tucked down in a corner where he was sheltered from the wind. He thought of just leaving the boy his privacy, but knew that he needed to talk, needed to cope with what had happened to him. Ravenwood sat near him and waited for the crying to pass. Soon enough, Bobby smelled the cigar and scrubbed at his face, tying to dry it, but only making it red and irritated. Passing him a handkerchief, Ravenwood said, "Dry your face, Bobby or it will freeze like that."

"Now, what brings you out of the house on such a fine day as this," he asked reasonably. It was not a fine day. The temperature was below zero; the snow still piled everywhere, and probably would not melt until spring. It was already spring. It had been a spring blizzard. Did that make it any better, that the snow would melt any sooner? No, no, it didn't. He didn't care if the snow never melted again. Everyone knew what had happened to him.

"Everyone knows what my father did to me," Bobby finally blurted.

"Do they actually know or do they suspect, or do you just assume they know because of something they do," asked Ravenwood.

Bobby looked at him blankly. Ravenwood reached out and cupped the boy's head with his hand. He did not attempt to draw Bobby to him. The boy might interpret that badly. Let him move on his own time. Bobby soon buried his head against Ravenwood's hip and just wailed. Once he quieted, then they could talk. Might help the boy, might not.

"Sometimes we just assume we know what's in people's heads. We usually make it worse than it really is."

"So they may not know what he did?" asked Bobby hopefully.

"They probably have some idea, Bobby. You did attack him, calling him some pretty descriptive names while you did it," said Ravenwood.

"Yea," agreed Bobby with a heavy sigh. "Yeah, I did. I shouldn't have done that, huh?"

"You definitely needed to do it, but maybe not so publicly. We can't take it back, just learn for the future," explained Ravenwood. "Now, there are some pretty good smells coming out of that kitchen. Why don't we go check them out?"

"OK," said Bobby As they started around the house, Brynna blocked their way.

"Where have you been?" she demanded of Bobby. "Mama made the most marvelous stuff." As she was talking, she was pulling apart the 'stuff' she carried and tucking a piece into Bobby's mouth. "Mama says it's called Monkey Bread. She doesn't know why. Isn't it good?"

Bobby just nodded, his mouth being full. "Do you want a piece, Da? It's so good and mama says it's easy. Next time I get to help and…"

"Brynna, take a deep breath. Hold it. Now let it out slowly. Not everyone functions at the speed of light. You need to slow down," said Ravenwood with a laugh.

"Mama says my heels are bouncing," explained Brynna.

"Did mama explain what the expression meant?" asked Ravenwood curiously, taking a piece of the monkey bread. "She said I have so much energy that it's overflowing out of my body and causing me to bounce on my heels when I'm not moving," explained Brynna.

"That's a pretty good description of your normal state," said Ravenwood, smiling.

"Mama said that too," said Brynna.

"Smart woman, your ma," agreed Ravenwood. "Why don't you two put on your boots and go bounce in the snow."

"OK," they both shouted and took off for the mudroom.

"Ravenwood," said Kate from behind him.

"Damn, woman. Do not do that. The least you can do is to make some noise," said Ravenwood after his body stopped twitching.

"Pot calling the kettle black and I make lots of noise, "said Kate, sliding her arms around his waist from behind and hugging him close. "You were just distracted by the children."

"I think you've learned how to just appear out of thin air," said Ravenwood.

"But the air is very thick today. Maybe I need thick air to appear," argued Kate.

"No such thing as thick air in the mountains," said Ravenwood. "Have you done your exercises for the day?"

"Not entirely. I thought you could walk with me if you don't walk too fast," said Kate.

"But my heels are bouncing," said Ravenwood. "Isn't that what you explained to Brynna?"

"Yes, it is. You just control your heels and walk with me. What did you do with her and Bobby," asked Kate.

"I told them to play in the snow. That should make them tired enough to stay on the ground," explained Ravenwood.

"Oh, yes, that should do it," agreed Kate.

"Are you serious," asked Ravenwood.

"About what," asked Kate distractedly?

"About them bouncing on their heels and maybe floating away,"

"I didn't say anything about floating away. What are you talking about?" She suddenly stopped. She looked at him. She tilted his face down so she could see his eyes, "The gods will punish you for teasing me," she said gravely.

Ravenwood exploded in laughter, and Kate joined him. They stood there on the font porch, their arms around each other, laughing like children.

Charlie and Gully heard it over at the woodshop and stopped to listen. Mr. Po heard it in the kitchen and stopped to listen. Brynna and Bobby heard it and ran to them to dance around the two of them, joining in the laughter.

Life continued smoothly for a while. Kate continued her exercises and her hip improved. She got the results from Dr. Raab's tests and was disappointed. Dr. Raab suggested either the Mayo Clinic or Johns Hopkins for further tests. The Mayo was closer so Dr. Raab set up an appointment with someone he trusted. Now it was Kate's turn for her heels to bounce. She was so nervous she moved constantly. One night in bed, Ravenwood asked her what was wrong, what was making her so afraid.

"I'm afraid that they will tell me there is nothing they can do to fix my head," said Kate.

"Would that be so bad," asked Ravenwood. "You'd still have the children and the valley, and me. Would that be so bad?"

"Would I," asked Kate.

"Would you what?" responded Ravenwood, not understanding her question.

"Would I still have the children, and the valley, and you, even if they can't fix my head?" said Kate. ""

"Oh, yes, my little cat. You cannot get rid of me so easily as that. You are my woman and I will keep you if I have to tie you to a fence post to keep you from floating away."

Kate wound her arms around his chest and curled close. "I will not float away."

"No matter how the tests turn out?" questioned Ravenwood.

"No matter what the test results say," assured Kate.

"Then why are you so worried, honey? If there is something they can fix, we'll do that. If there is nothing they can do, it makes no difference to us and we will continue on," said Ravenwood.

"So, you are saying taking the tests has no downside?" said Kate.

"No downside," agreed Ravenwood. "Now can you relax?"

"Not really," said Kate.

"Oh, we can find a way," assured Ravenwood.

As she laughed, she felt the tension begin to leave her body. As he began to lick, suck, and stroke, a different kind of tension took its place and Kate welcomed it. Her body and her mind responded completely to him and she lay back and allowed him to work his magic for her. He was, after all, such a talented magician.

Several hours later, as they both floated a few feet above the mattress, Kate still had questions, but no energy to ask them, so she just curled against Ravenwood and held on to the most solid thing in her world. Everything else was so fluid it was difficult to grasp. Her world had shifted at light speed with the blizzard and finding the children and bringing them here. Now she must hold on to this world and make it her own. Yes, she would go to the clinic. Yes, she would take their tests. Yes, she would listen to their results. No, it would not devastate her and it would not defeat her. With this in mind, she went to sleep. In the morning, she would have a little magic of her own for Ravenwood, and he did so enjoy a good magic show.

They went to the clinic. She took all the tests. How did she do? That's an interesting question. The doctors were fascinated, but not alarmed. The results showed no physical problem they could fix. More importantly, she did not score in what they considered their 'defined normal range' on the verbal part of the test. Kate had quite a lot to say about their 'defined normal range' and none of it was good. She had even more to say about the medical community as a whole. It was also not good. Once she had the results of her original tests, the doctors outlined the additional tests they would like to do, what they were for, how long they would take, and how much they would cost.

How did Kate respond to their proposals? With all the words at her command, with all her considerable practice at leading teams and persuading people – how did she respond to the doctor's pitch? For that, is how she saw it – as a pitch and what was her response?

"Hmgph!" she said emphatically. It was such an expressive word, combining both disgust and disbelief. She wondered how she got by without it all these years.

Then they went home. The children were delighted. Everyone else was thrilled. No one behaved as though there was anything wrong with her. If they had, Ravenwood would probably have wrung their neck, but the people accepted her as they had met her and that was after her accident, after her fall. She had just a slight limp and it improved almost daily. Soon it would be gone. Ravenwood wanted to marry and she had promised to do it when she no longer limped down the aisle. She understood that it was important for the children. Still, she hesitated.

It would be to give up her freedom once more. She had done it so many times over the years, in so many different ceremonies, that it should be no big deal, but it was. She wasn't exactly sure why it was, but it was. Ravenwood sensed this and did not push. He had made it clear that he wanted to marry and now she must come to it on her own. The marriage would make no difference in their daily lives and they both knew that, but the small children would not believe that she was truly going to stay until she adopted them. That was the signal. It meant they were safe, were part of a family, and they were wanted.

The spring had turned to summer and Kate learned the joys of swimming in the basin. It was a large rock pool not too far from the house. Its sides were so smooth, like a big scoop pulled from the rock while it was still hot. Fields of wild flowers and fir trees surrounded the basin. After swimming, if they were alone, they would make love in those fields with the trees nodding above and their scent drifting on the wind. The summer passed as the children played, dreamed, and worked with their parents. Three colts were born that year and the buyers swamped the farm each time to get a look at the animal and check its breeding. Ravenwood negotiated the sales, sometimes for a fixed price up front, sometimes for a share of any future winnings. The latter was always a gamble, but when it paid off, it paid off big.

"Why does Ravenwood negotiate the sales?" asked Kate one evening.

"Ravenwood handles the money for all of us," replied Jonas.

"Handles it for all of you? For all the various businesses? Why?" asked Kate.

"Because he's bloody good at it," said Gully bluntly.

"Oh, aye, Joe's a talent for the horses. Charlie and I have a talent for the wood. Mr. Po has a talent for his lotions and potions and cooking and Jonas has a talent for the law. Ravenwood has a talent for the money, which keeps everything tucked up nice and tight. Very important is that talent, very important, "Gully explained.

Later that night as they lay in bed, Kate said to Ravenwood, "Gully says you have a talent for the money."

"Gully has a big mouth," said Ravenwood softly.

"Don't be angry with him. After all, I asked. It's not like you're an open book or anything."

Ravenwood chuckled, turned her face up to his, and said gravely, "Neither are you, honey. Neither are you."

Kate responded with a radiant smile, which rolled over Ravenwood like the sun breaking over the mountains in the mornings. The oddest compliments thrilled her. That was good because he gave the oddest compliments of any man, or so the women told him. This was only a compliment when it applied to Kate. As she frequently said, her head worked differently now.

Some things worked like before – mostly. Some things did not work at all. Some things were new. Overall, she had some trouble adjusting, but Ravenwood knew many people who were good with the details. He had an entire house full who knew the schedules and the appointments, who were supposed to be doing what and when; including him. Kate touched a different chord in all of them. She knew where the children were and if they were all right. She knew if something had gone wrong in the valley. She called it a change in energy. It was like a different language to him. It was not always clear, but he had learned to pay attention. No matter how distracted she seemed, there was always something worth knowing at the bottom. Something that triggered a response in her was always worth the attention.

They had settled into something of a routine. Jonas woke the children. Mr. Po fixed their breakfast. Jamie took them down to the bus stop. He and Kate woke when they woke. It was usually early. He could not break that habit after so many years. He took his coffee and went to work in the study, reading financial information, making investments for the family, checking investments he had already made, adjusting as necessary.

She baked on Mondays. After the weekend, every crumb was gone. She was quite good now. As the summer fruit came in, the whole family worked it up. Mr. Po made jams and jellies. Kate made cobblers. The family was not much on cake, but they did love a good cobbler. They had fresh ones through the summer and the freezer was full. It just required going from the freezer to the oven, and they had fresh cobbler through the winter. She had done the same with their favorite bread. She always mixed extra loaves and they were in the freezer, ready to bake whenever needed. This all happened smoothly unless one of the mares was ready to foal.

Then everyone reported to the barn to assist. Joe had given the heavy work over to Ravenwood and they discovered early on that Kate had the ability to calm the mare during the birthing. Sara had this ability in a different way, but the effect was the same. The mares remained calm. The births were easier. The foals were healthier. Joe did not even pretend know what it was she did. Jamie, who had been on the receiving end when he hurt his leg, called it 'The sound you cannot quite hear – The vibration you cannot quite feel.' What he knew was that it made him feel good. He had pain, but was not overwhelmed. He had energy, but no panic. He felt her strength flowing into him and he did not know how else to describe it, but it worked really well. Kate didn't know what to call it either. She said it was one of the new things. They finally settled on calling it the Touch, for lack of anything more descriptive.

The children were not happy with the plans Kate and Ravenwood made for their wedding. They wanted a proper wedding and they wanted to attend. So did everyone else. A simple ceremony with a justice of the peace would not do. Kate and Ravenwood had been planning to keep it low key; a simple ceremony followed by a family dinner at home. This met all their requirements, but there were many people to consider in this family. Kate wondered how Ravenwood felt about it.

"Ravenwood, how would you feel about having a wedding here at the house with a minister and a photographer with a nice dress and a suit and all like that?" asked Kate.

"He was silent for a moment and then said, "We can have anything you want, but we have the oath tonight under the moon. It's at its fullest tonight and thats when it needs to be done."

He quirked his eyebrow in question and she nodded agreement. She would work on the wedding plans. They would do the blood oath tonight. She knew she needed nothing special for the oath except some clean cloths to wipe any excess blood, but what kind of dress could she be married in -certainly not one of those little white frou-frou things. She would have to talk to Lena. She could make anything, or so everyone said.

That evening, after the children were in bed and the men sat smoking on the porch, Ravenwood led her toward the basin in silence. He built a small fire to heat the knife. There would be no witnesses to the oath. For thousands of years, long before the coming of the church and its Christian doctrines, this oath bound a man and woman together. The blood would bind them closer, deeper than any words that the priest could say. It was the old way of bonding to a mate and they both knew it well.

The knife was ready. Ravenwood took it and sliced lightly cross his left palm, just enough to draw a thin line of blood. Then he held out his hand for hers. She placed her hand in his, palm up and open for the blade. He moved quickly to blood her palm and then clasping their two bleeding hands together between their bodies; he placed his other arm around her back and held her close.

"Blood of my blood," intoned Kate, looking into his face.

"Bone of my bone," responded Ravenwood.

"Breath of my breath," they said together, their lips touching deeply to seal the oath.

The lightening cracked and the energy of the universe moved through them. It was always the same, always powerful and beautiful. The rain began gently. As they unclasped their hands, they saw that the shallow cuts bled no more. Only a faint red line remained on both their palms to show where the cut had been.

As they undressed and slid into the basin, a feeling of wild freedom washed over Kate. She had never known this freedom. This was different. It had no boundaries. It reached forever.

She drifted in the water, knowing that Ravenwood was keeping watch and he would not let her drown. How marvelously they fit together. As her legs circled his waist while her hair floated on the water, she thought again of all the people they had been and wondered who they would be.

The dogs coming up from the house broke the dreamlike quality. Beau and Sheba circled the basin, sniffing and checking for foreign odors. Ravenwood watched them closely. They were a good clue to strangers. They knew the family by sight and smell and would alert on any strangers, but they found none tonight and moved on down to the house, satisfied that they had done their job.

Sex in the water was both easy and exciting. It flowed naturally between them, as from long practice. Relaxing on the apron of the basin afterward, Kate wondered again how she had found this life and this man. Whatever it had been, she gave silent thanks.

"Will we be married here at the house? I think it would be better than church," said Kate.

"Yes, we can be married here. Who do we invite," asked Ravenwood.

"The family and the priest," replied Kate.

"And the photographer?" questioned Ravenwood.

"And the photographer," agreed Kate. "The children want a wedding picture."

"Is that what this is about? The children feeling left out if we just went and did it?" asked Ravenwood..

"They were pretty specific in their complaint," said Kate.

"All of them? They showed up as a group?" queried Ravenwood, wanting specifics.

"Yes, they showed up as a group. They wanted a proper ceremony and a proper picture," said Kate. "Their words - That's what you get for sending them to Catholic school."

"It's the best school in the state. Don't give a hang what organization controls it. They get a good education." He said with a smile.

"We need to pick a date. We need to run it by Joe to make sure it's OK. You need to talk to the priest. I need to get a dress. The children have to have clothes. Do they have clothes for a wedding? Do you have a suit?" Kate's voice was moving quicker and her words clicked through the list of things that needed doing.

Ravenwood pulled her over on top of him and kissed her hard, "Don't get your knickers in a twist, woman. It will work fine. Yes, I have a suit. Yes, the children have dress clothes. Yes, we can have the wedding at the house. Pick a date and get yourself a dress. I kind of fancy you in green this time; something sleek and slim."

"And here I was thinking about that white lace gown with the long sleeves and flowing train," said Kate with a grin.

Ravenwood groaned.

If you're goanna be ill, I'm out of here," Kate yelped sitting up quickly; at least she tried to sit up.

Ravenwood just tightened his arm around her waist and looked at her as though to ask what she thought she was doing and where she thought she was going.

"I'll see what I can find. I thought I could talk to Lena. She might have some ideas," said Kate.

"Let me know. I have things I need to take care of," requested Ravenwood.

"What things?" demanded Kate?

He just lifted the corner of his mouth in a smile and ignored her question. Just as she took a deep breath and prepared to question him further, he stood up. Lifting her with him and holding her clothes in one hand, he asked, "Do you want to wear any of those back to the house or are you comfortable the way you are?"

Kate grabbed her jeans and t-shirt out of his hand and began pulling them on, stuffing the underwear in her pocket. She crammed her feet into the moccasins she had worn over to the basin and began walking toward the house.

Ravenwood was also dressed by this time and took her hand as he joined her on the walk home.

"How does the first Saturday in October sound for a wedding?" asked Ravenwood. That gives you about a month for the dress and Mr. Po for the meal. If we need a proper ceremony and a proper picture, don't we need a proper cake?"

"Yes, but I don't think I can bake a wedding cake. I don't think it's a good idea. I…" Kate began to stutter.

"Honey, no one is asking you to bake your own wedding cake," said Ravenwood. "I thought we would ask Mrs. Franks. She does most of the local wedding cakes."

"Have I met Mrs. Franks," asked Kate.

"No idea, but that can be fixed, OK?"

"OK."

They finished their walk in silence, friendly silence. After all, they had just finished the blood oath, and were planning their wedding. Friends were the best thing that could be. It was what they had always valued most. The thing that would last the longest was the friendship.

The next day, Jonas drove her over to Lena's to see what they could do about a dress. Ravenwood went to talk to the priest and then to Mrs. Franks; and then he went to see the judge. Father Killner did not wish to perform the ceremony at the farm. Truth was, he did not wish to perform the ceremony at all. He had never really approved of the Ravenwoods and certainly not Ravenwood himself. He considered the whole clan immoral, undisciplined, and wild. He was constantly amazed that the little children were well behaved, studious, and polite. He prayed that they stayed that way, but the wedding should take place in church, not in somebody's yard.

Fortunately, Big Bill Kostner did not have any such hang-ups and readily agreed to perform the ceremony on the first Saturday in October. "Bless you both. I thought you would never get those kids a mama. I will be there with bells on. Thank the gods you're out of the competition, since you've already got the best looking woman in the state." Big Bill shook his hand heartily, clapped him on the shoulder, and was a happy man.

He thought about dropping by Lena's on his way home, but decided that would probably send both women into fits. Besides, Jonas had strict orders to grab a swatch of whatever fabric Kate settled on for the dress. He needed to talk to Cassandra St. John. He had never met her. He knew she had a small place out past the school and Stella said she was a very talented jewelry designer and could make anything Ravenwood wanted.

He was thinking earrings. He already had the stones. He knew she preferred hoops, but that was about it. Cassie would need to do the design. He hoped she could. If he had to go with one of the jewelry design firms in the capitol, he would never make the wedding date. She sold some of her work at the Emporium. Stella had shown him some of Cassie's work. He liked what he saw and hoped they could reach terms.

As Cassie looked through the peephole, she saw a large, well kept, but intimidating man. She remembered his voice from the phone call and felt that it suited him well. She hesitated only a moment, then pulled herself together and opened the door. Once again, he liked what he saw. Cassie was about 5 foot 10 or so, with dark red hair and golden eyes. She invited him to her workroom and they began their negotiations. Ravenwood explained what he wanted, 18k or higher for the gold and he brought the stones with him. Kate preferred hoops, but since he wanted her to wear them often, the stones had to be secure and there had to be an extra safety on the clasp so she wouldn't fear losing them.

"Ravenwood, these are green diamonds," said Cassie. "These are natural green diamonds. Where did you get natural green diamonds?"

"From a friend of a friend of a... You know how it goes. Can you work with them," he asked.

"Can I? Oh, yes. These are the most beautiful stones I've ever seen." She did a rough sketch of her thoughts about the earrings. They agreed on when she would provide the finished sketch for his approval. He went on his way. There was nothing more that needed doing today so he arrived at the bus stop in time to pick up the children and take them back up to the house. All except Jamie, who had football practice, Mr. Po had snacks for his returning scholars before they tackled their homework. Ravenwood had a few questions before they dug in.

"Why did you feel it was so important to have a proper wedding? What about just having a civil ceremony did not strike you as proper," asked Ravenwood.

"It's not whether it's a civil or religious ceremony, it's that there is a ceremony," explained Luc and Trist alternately.

"It's a good thing you don't care whether it's a religious ceremony. Your mother and I want to be married here at the house. Father Killner refuses to perform the ceremony outside a church," said Ravenwood.

"He just doesn't like you, Da," said Sela. The bark of his laugh echoed sharply in the kitchen and he ruffled her hair.

"So, who is doing the ceremony," asked Gabe.

"Big Bill," said Ravenwood. "He is a happy man."

"I'll just bet his is," said Luc.

"A lot less competition," said Trist.

"Maybe he'll finally find some woman who can put up with him."

"Doubt it."

"Did I know we were in competition for women?" asked Ravenwood looking back and forth between the boys.

"Da, every man in the state considers you competition."

Ravenwood's look went from surprise to amusement to extreme satisfaction. He had come out the winner, even if he didn't know they were competing. Any man who ended up with Kate was definitely the winner.

He wondered how Kate was doing with her dress. He wondered if Jonas would survive the process. Good thing there was cell phone reception over at Lena's so he could do some work while he waited.

"Jonas, what do you think of this print?" asked Kate.

"It's a bit gaudy for a wedding, Kate," replied Jonas. "So you've run through all the regular, normal materials and now you're on to the esoteric and exotic. Is that it? Are you looking for something special or just something different? Does it need to be unique or does it need to be shocking? What's the objective here?" demanded Jonas.

"You've been very patient, Jonas and I appreciate it," said Kate, "but don't blow it now. We're almost done."

"OK, OK," said Jonas, taking a deep breath and holding up his hands in surrender.

Suddenly, the very material she had been searching for appeared. It was a subtle green and gold print on a lovely watered silk. It flowed. It draped. It was green. With the right dress pattern, it would also be sleek and slim.

"Here you are, dear," said Lena. "You will look fantastic in this pattern. Not so many women could carry it off. It does lie close to the body but for someone with your build, that shouldn't be a problem."

When they matched the pattern with the silky material, they both knew it was magic. The dress would be fantastic. She was going to need shoes, not just shoes, but heels. It probably wouldn't be a good idea to take Jonas on that shopping trip. He just might explode, or was implode the correct word? Many people at the ranch could drive. She could drive if she had to, but they learned early on that she just couldn't maintain her concentration; so she wandered off the road, she wandered into the ditch; it was dangerous to let your mind wander when driving in the mountains.

Besides, Ravenwood seemed to think it was important that someone always be with her. He said she never saw the danger, that she didn't really understand how men worked. That was true. She wasn't very good at it. Good thing Ravenwood didn't require much of it. Good thing she didn't either. Such a pair they were, but that was all right. She knew she used to enjoy driving, but now it just took too much work. Besides, so many others could do it better. Why not let them while they were willing.

Shoes, she repeated to herself. Where did she find shoes in this town? She might as well start at the Emporium. If Stella did not have them, she would know where to get them. That could wait for another day. She was tired. Maybe she could sleep on the drive home.

"Miss Kate, Miss Kate. Honey, you need to stand up straight now. We need to fit this pattern and the only way its going to look right is if you stand up and pay attention," said Lena sharply.

"Yes, ma'am," replied Kate. She knew that she had begun to wander in her mind and Lena was just getting her attention and helping her focus.

"Now, honey, when are you going to need this dress?" asked Lena.

"The first Saturday in October," replied Kate.

"Why that's less than a month away," protested Lena.

'I know," said Kate.

"We should have the preliminary fitting next week. I'll get everything cut and stitched and then we can make adjustments. I like to make a practice garment in cotton before I use the silk, but there's not really time for that," said Lena, looking hopefully at Kate.

"No, sorry," said Kate cheerfully. "We're having a wedding regardless of what I am wearing. Ravenwood does not have much patience about these things."

Jonas just smiled. He knew his father had no patience for this process and he didn't care whether Kate had a dress or went naked. Well, he did care if she went to her wedding naked. There were, after all, other people at the ceremony.

As Kate began to stroll outside, Jonas explained to Lena that he needed a swatch of the fabric for Ravenwood. Lena kept right on talking to Kate as she followed her outside and tucked the fabric swatch in Jonas pocket without missing a word.

"Lena, is there a good place in town to get shoes? I mean a pair of pumps to go with my dress," asked Kate, hopefully.

"Emporium's got most everything, and what she ain't got, she'll get double quick. Now what color shoes were you thinking," asked Lena.

"I was thinking a British Tan in a nice 2, maybe 2.5 inch heel. I'll have to practice walking in them. I never was very good," explained Kate.

"Then you'd best check with Stella as soon as possible. Here now, you take a sample of the fabric with you and make sure the shoe color looks good," said Lena, smiling mischievously at Jonas.

"Kate, we're not really going to do shoes today are we? I already sat through the dress pattern picking and the fabric choosing and the..." said Jonas somewhat plaintively as Kate held her finger across his lips to silence him.

"Tomorrow will be soon enough," said Kate serenely.

Heaving a sigh of relief, Jonas headed for home. They drove in silence for a while. Jonas finally spoke.

"I'm really glad you're marrying Ravenwood, Kate. It's good for him. Hell, it's good for all of us."

"Thank you, Jonas. It's always important to have the entire family in sync when it comes to those things. Always important," said Kate.

"You're not nervous are your, Kate," asked Jonas.

"No, Jonas, not nervous," responded Kate with a soft smile.

"Than what are you thinking?" asked Jonas.

"Who I'm going to torture tomorrow," answered Kate serenely.

"What kind of torture are you planning, Kate?"

"Shoe shopping," explained Kate.

Jonas began to laugh. It had been a while since he had a good belly laugh and he thoroughly enjoyed this one.

"Do you think you can say that in any more innocent a tone," he asked.

"No," Kate replied.

"Are we going to be home in time for supper," asked Kate.

"Should be about 45 minutes now," replied Jonas. "But that's only if you stop making me laugh so hard I can't control the car," said Jonas.

"Hmgph," replied Kate.

"You picked that up quick enough," observed Jonas.

It's a good expression. I like it. But it s difficult to spell," said Kate.

Jonas just looked over at her confusedly, wondering why she would even try to spell it. "Jonas, don't think about it too hard," he said to himself. He never talked to himself. Next thing you knew he would be mumbling and drooling. Well, maybe not drooling, but definitely mumbling. I wonder if Ravenwood actually knows what he is in for thought Jonas. As he looked over at Kate, her eyes closed and she looked so peaceful. Then she reached out and touched his wrist. That feeling of sweet peace flooded through him and all was right with his world, at least for now.

She had answered his question, even though he had not asked it aloud. Now that was spooky. It was actually a little beyond spooky. What was the word for beyond spooky? There must be one.

Kate curled her hand back into her lap and continued to doze. When they reached the farm, he secretly handed Ravenwood the small piece of fabric. He was surprised to see the corner of his mouth kick up in what passed for a smile.

"Its perfect," murmured Ravenwood.

Jonas walked back to the house. He needed to clear his head. He needed a stiff drink or a swift kick. He wasn't sure which would be more effective, maybe both, maybe neither. OK, don't think too hard on it. It will make you crazy. As he approached the house, he saw Joe rocking on the porch.

It was not that leisurely, casual rocking that told of everything being right with the world. No agitation and anger here either. It was somewhere in the middle. He was sure he would get the explanation in time. Right now, he continued past the house and on to Gram's grave. Talking to Gram was soothing. Had been when she was alive. Still was now that she was dead. Odd, that, but there it was. Here he had been, thinking about how spooky Kate's behavior was and he was in the side yard talking to a woman who had been dead for 3 years. Maybe the whole family needed a good shrink session. Not a one of them would actually cooperate, but it was a grand thought wasn't it.

Jonas sat by the grave and continued his conversation with Gram. He had not talked to her for a while, but he did not think she was lonely. The children were out here every few days, especially in the summer. He lay down and went to sleep. Some of their best conversations took place when he was asleep.

When he woke, he knew that he would take Kate shoe shopping. Gram said the day was too important to leave to chance, and couldn't he tell how different Ravenwood was since she had been here. Didn't he want it to continue? Then he needed to help, and that didn't mean he could whine about it later. She did not have any idea why Joe was agitated.

As Jonas went into the house via one of the back doors, he heard the children coming in the front. They tried to start a conversation with Joe as they passed, but he was unresponsive. Brynna might be a good source. She was still young for a full day of school. He found her in the sewing room. She found it an almost magical place. It was the most beautiful room in the house. Gram had been very particular about its decoration. She said you needed to surround yourself with beauty to create beauty. Here she created beauty with her yarns and threads, with her quilts and wall hangings. He remembered when they had first shown Kate this room; she claimed it immediately.

"Bryn," called Jonas from the doorway. "Bryn are you in here," he called as he walked into the room.

"Hi, Uncle Jon," said Bryn, bouncing up from behind the sofa.

"Bryn, did anything unusual happen today?" asked Jonas. Brynna began to giggle and dropped back onto the sofa.

"I'll take that as a yes," said Jonas. "Want to tell me what."

"Joe made me promise not to tell," said Brynna.

"Not to tell anybody or not to tell me?" asked Jonas, thinking that maybe he had a way around this promise.

"Not to tell anyone, but especially not the family," replied Brynna. Then she sat down on the sofa, took her favorite doll and began to rock. As she rocked, she talked to the doll.

"Wasn't it strange when that car full of women showed up wanting to marry Joe?" Brynna murmured to the doll. She definitely had Jonas' attention. He froze. He did not move and he did not speak. He didn't want to do anything that would distract her from her conversation. This had to be good.

"They thought since Ravenwood was finally getting married that they should make it a double wedding and Joe could marry one of them. They said he's been seeing each of them once a week for the past year and they think he should make up his mind," finished Brynna. Then she turned to face him over the back of the sofa.

"Uncle Jonas, you don't think he will actually do it, do you," asked Brynna?

"No, baby, I don't," Jonas assured her.

"Oh, good," said Brynna emphatically.

"Why," asked Jonas curiously? He had never seen Brynna react to any woman Joe dated, or he dated, or even Ravenwood dated, not until Kate arrived.

"I didn't like them. Arriving in their fancy car, being all dressed up, very impractical for the farm, talking to Gran as if he was even younger than I was. They were just prissy little bitches. Well, some of them weren't so little," announced Brynna, nodding her head for emphasis.

Jonas tried to control his laughter, and he did a good job - sort of.

"Brynna, we don't call people prissy little bitches," said Jonas.

"Even when they are?" asked Brynna.

"Especially when they are," said Jonas. "Prissy little bitches have long memories and a knack for getting even," he explained.

"Oh, that's bad. I didn't tell them they were prissy little bitches, and I didn't tell Gran. He already seemed too upset. I just told you," reasoned Brynna.

"That's good, baby. That's very good. Do not tell your brothers and sister. Let's not throw fuel on the fire," said Jonas.

Brynna just looked confused, but she agreed with his request. "Can I tell Da?" she asked at last.

"You can talk to him about it later, but I'll take care of letting him know, OK?" said Jonas. "Do you remember anything else about the women who showed up?" asked Jonas.

"You mean besides their names," asked Brynna.

"Their names would be good, "responded Jonas.

"Why," asked Brynna with that direct, no nonsense look she got from both her Grandmother and her mother.

"In case they decide to sue your granddad," Jonas replied, thinking quickly.

"Un huh," Brynna replied skeptically, "Right?"

With that, she hopped down from the sofa and went outside. She crawled onto Joe's lap and hugged him as he continued to rock. As Ravenwood crossed over the porch, he glanced at Joe once, then twice, then a third time before he opened his mouth to ask a question. Jonas came around the corner form the mudroom, motioning Ravenwood off the porch, as he kept moving. They were well away from the house when Ravenwood realized he was not crying, but laughing; not only laughing, laughing outrageously. Laying a hand on Jonas shoulder, Ravenwood brought him to a halt and spun him around.

"You appear to be entertained, Jonas. Want to share," asked Ravenwood?

"Yes sir, just dying to share. Probably bust something if I don't," said Jonas breathing hard and continuing to laugh.

"Speak," ordered Ravenwood sharply. Jonas pulled himself together and began to relay the story he got from Brynna.

"No wonder Joe looks slightly traumatized," said Ravenwood. "He's not used to that kind of behavior in women. Not used to women thinking of him like that. Wonder if they compared performance notes."

"Wonder if there's any more of them," said Jonas aloud. They had to get the answers to Jonas' question so they headed back to the house to speak to Joe.

Another car had arrived, the driver just getting out and heading to the porch.

"Oh, Joe, you poor man," she cried, hugging him close. "They told me what they did this morning. That was so unfair," she cried.

Joe looked shell-shocked. He didn't know whether to stand up or spit and there was definitely a debate going on in his head.

Ravenwood didn't know if she was a current member of the club or just looking to join now that the others had gathered against Joe. Either way, she needed to go. Then he thought maybe Joe night want to keep her, since his other women were on the outs with him.

"Clarissa, we've had quite a lot of drama for the morning. Is there something I can do for you," asked Ravenwood?

"I thought Joe could use some comfort, now that his other women have mutinied against him," explained Clarissa, patting her hair, and her cheek, and her hip. Lord knew what she would have patted next, but Kate came out the front door. She was carrying Brynna, who had her legs firmly wrapped around her mama's waist and her head buried in Kate's shoulder. This was odd. Brynna was too big for Kate to carry. She and Ravenwood had come to an understanding about this several months ago.

Kate tucked Brynna down on Joe's lap.

"So Clarissa, moving in for the kill?" inquired Kate.

"I don't know what you're talking about, Kate. You know I've always cared for Joe," protested Clarissa.

Ravenwood and Jonas took seats on the porch railing. Joe looked more than a little ill.

"And I know you've always been slightly on the outside of his circle," said Kate.

"But no more," said Clarissa. "His circle, as you call it, is no more."

"They'll be back," said Kate. All the men looked somewhat surprised. Clarissa looked shocked.

"You can't possibly believe they would come back to him after the ultimatum they laid down. Who would crawl like that?" jeered Clarissa.

"Oh, and you are doing what, exactly?" asked Kate.

"I didn't make any demands. I didn't make any threats. I haven't asked him for a thing and..."

"Not yet you haven't. Wait for it."

"Enough," said Joe, erupting from his chair. He jumped to his feet. His voice echoed down the porch.

"Go from this valley and don't come back. Go now!" ordered Joe sternly.

Clarissa looked like she was about to protest, but then looked at Kate and said her goodbyes. They watched her all the way out the gate. Then Kate turned to Joe and, giving his a huge hug and a kiss on the cheek, she said," I'm so glad you are back, Joe."

"Back, back from where? I haven't been anywhere," said Joe.

"But you have," said Kate. "The visit from those PLBs this morning traumatized you and you quite needed a delaying action until your brain worked its way through it."

"Sis, as usual, I have no idea what you're saying, but that's all right. What's a PLB?" asked Joe.

"Prissy Little Bitch," answered Jonas, glaring directly at Brynna.

"Don't look at me like that. Gran needed help so I went to get mama," said Brynna defiantly.

"I thought we had a deal. I thought you were going to let me handle it. I can be pretty good in a verbal jousting match, you know," reasoned Jonas.

"It wasn't your kind of fight," said Brynna, trotting inside. "Mr. Po, do we have any food," she called as she passed down the front hall. It was frightening, how much she sounded like Kate.

"What did she mean it wasn't my kind of fight?" asked Jonas.

Ravenwood just shrugged one shoulder saying, "It's done now. Need to move on."

"I still need shoes," said Kate.

Shoes?" asked Joe.

"I'll take you tomorrow," said Jonas.

"Really?" asked Kate. "You'll take me?"

"Yes," said Jonas. "We can't have Ravenwood getting a look at the wedding shoes. Wouldn't do – Just wouldn't do - Bad luck all over the place."

"Thank you, Jonas," said Kate, planting a kiss on his cheek. Kate followed Brynna inside and closed the door.

"So, how many women have you been seeing lately," asked Jonas.

"Hmgph," replied Joe.

"Brynna named at least 5, maybe 6. She says they all arrived together."

"No secret I been seeing them. Ain't found another woman like your Ma," he nodded at Ravenwood. "Don't expect to. Only woman who's as strong is your Kate. It's a rare combination: strength, beauty, intelligence. Your ma had it, so does Kate. Brought peace to your eyes, she has, first time since you were a boy. I thought I'd never see it again."

Ravenwood just tilted his head and looked at him; them wrapped his arms around Joe's shoulders and hugged him hard. Joe patted Ravenwood's back in thanks and started down the front steps.

"That's more than enough drama for the day. More than enough for the entire month," said Joe.

"Kate calls it Sturm und Drang," Ravenwood said with a laugh, following Joe down the steps.

"Who and what?" asked Joe.

"I don't remember exactly, but Jonas is a bright young attorney. Surely he knows what Sturm und Drang is."

"Something to be avoided if you want to retain your sanity," replied Jonas, and with that, the three men moved down the road leading to the barn. Kate and Brynna watched them from the upstairs window.

"Good. They would go to the barn. Hard, physical work did wonders after that kind of emotion." Kate barely realized she was speaking to Brynna, teaching her the insights she would use for the rest of her life.

Early the next morning, Kate and Brynna climbed into Jonas' truck for the ride to town and the infamous shoe-shopping trip. Jonas had armed himself with legal work to get through several hours and a novel to supplement that.

"Brynna, please sit down and fasten your seat belt," said Kate.

"Yes, mama," replied Brynna, and she did sit down. She did fasten her seat belt. She did not stop moving. Her whole body seemed to radiate energy. It ripped through the truck, catching everyone in its flow. They began their shoe shopping expedition at the Emporium. They finished in half an hour and were on their way home, the perfect shoes tucked securely at Kate's feet. Jonas was stunned.

"Kate, do you always find shoes that easily," asked Jonas.

"No, but sometimes you just get lucky," replied Kate.

"Lucky? You tried on three pair of shoes. It took less than half an hour. That's not luck. That's a miracle," said Jonas.

"No, Just a bonus," said Kate.

"Bonus?" queried Jonas.

"Um hmm," said Kate sleepily. Brynna curled on the seat, her head in Kate's lap. It sounded like Kate would join her soon.

Kate and Brynna slept most of the way back to the ranch. It was peaceful in the truck. It was peaceful in the house. Hell, it was peaceful in the entire valley. Kate woke up as they came through the gate. She was excited about the wedding. It was her first in this life. It was not so important on the grand list of universal things. She knew she would be with Ravenwood whether they were married or not. She knew it would make no difference in their daily lives. Still, it was exciting. Mr. PO was already forming his menu. They were planning some sort of decorations for the side porch, where the ceremony would take place. She could feel the ripples of energy running up and down the valley. By the time of the wedding, they would arch over the valley, filling the sky with their effect. It was sort of like a giant orgasm, and Kate was right at the center of the quake.

"Joe, did you promise any of these women anything that might give them grounds to sue you," asked Jonas later that day?

"Not unless the promise of good, healthy, regular sex is grounds," said Joe.

"That was it – just sex: No talk of tomorrow together, No talk of trips together, nothing they could have construed as a promise?" Jonas asked, pushing his Grandfather to remember anything he might have said that could have been misinterpreted.

"What are you on about, boy? Is one of those women claiming I promised them something more?" asked Joe.

"No sir. Not one, all," replied Jonas.

"All? All of them, said Joe, his indignation ringing through the house, and the barn, and bouncing off the mountains that surrounded the valley. "What are they claiming I promised them?"

"Marriage, of course," said Jonas.

"Hmgph," responded Joe in disgust. Now he thought long and hard. Had he said anything they could have misinterpreted. Had he teased a bit when they were playing? Had he implied that any of them had any kind of possible position in his life other than a comforting lover? No. No, he had given them no reason for this.

"Jonas, we need to fight this. Can you handle it or do we need a trial lawyer," asked Joe.

"We need a trial lawyer. I can do a lot of the prep work, but if it goes to trial, we need someone with more experience," said Jonas.

"All right, how far are they going to push it and who do we need," asked Joe.

"They are gonna push it as far and as hard as possible. We aren't going to settle so it's definitely going to trial," said Jonas

"Who do we need?" asked Joe.

"We need Emily Raintree,"said Jonas. "I'll give her a call. She probably knows already. News travels fast in the legal community."

"She'll be entertained as hell. I can see it now," said Joe.

"She's probably wondering how you kept 5 women sexually satisfied for 2 years without keeling over, "observed Ravenwood.

"Keeling over?" asked Joe.

"Exhaustion, Joe. Contrary to popular myth, most men don't have sex every night. They certainly don't have sex with a different woman in a different house every night. They are gonna be all over this one and you have to be prepared to speak openly about it," explained Jonas.

"I don't like it, but I'll do what needs to be done," said Joe, who sighed deeply as he walked the porch. It wasn't right that they wanted to sue him, wasn't right at all. You tried to be nice to some people. He had benefited too, no doubt about that, but overall, he had tried to give them a warmth and affection that they no longer had. This was how they said thank you. You just couldn't please some people. He would go talk to Sara. He told her everything. She knew all about the women. It had been well over a year after Sara's death before he had any interest in talking to or seeing any woman. Sara pointed out that he could help these women. She got him past his block, and it worked. It worked really well. The women were happy. He was happy. What slithered into their world and planted ideas, ideas that had obviously taken root and flourished. Something seemed off. He needed to speak to Ravenwood. That boy could smell a plot a mile away – and there was something smelly here.

Kate stood looking over the valley, a slight frown on her face. She looked the full length of the valley. She smelled the wind. She felt it touch her cheek and lift her hair, and she frowned.

"Ravenwood, something is not right here," announced Kate.

"How not right?" asked Ravenwood.

"I don't know exactly, but the energy of the valley is disturbed like, like…." Kate stuttered in confusion.

"Like we got a snake in the garden," said Joe.

"Exactly," Kate agreed.

Ravenwood looked hard at his father, then at Kate, then back at his father.

"Guess we better find some poison that won't kill the dogs," said Ravenwood.

"What's he talking about?" asked Jonas.

"I don't know exactly, but I'm sure it will be fine," said Kate.

"Joe, what is going on?" asked Jonas.

"Too much of a coincidence, them all getting their knickers in a twist at the same time, on the same subject, way too much. Must be someone driving it. Question is, who?" said Joe.

"Bigger question is why," corrected Ravenwood.

They moved quietly, fanning out from the valley, asking seemingly casual questions. It took about a week to gather the info, a few days to correlate the data, and the trend line popped immediately. At least Kate saw it immediately. It took the others a little longer, but they finally had to admit – they want our valley. Now we need to determine who exactly they are.

As they discussed the problem of whom, they worked their way backward through what had seemed like random, meaningless events. They were looking for the driver. Jonas; meanwhile, was helping Emily get the marriage minded women's case thrown out of court.

"All these little incidents, I never noticed, I never saw it," said Joe sadly.

"None of us did. They hid it well," said Ravenwood.

"How long ago did it start?" asked Joe.

"About 3 months. Who was new on the scene 3 months ago?" asked Gully.

"That fancy new District Attorney they brought in from the city. Nasty business, that. Threw Simon Raintree out of a job that he did really well," said Joe.

"Spread rumors that he couldn't be trusted. He wasn't American," added Jonas.

"Translation is – he wasn't white," explained Charlie.

"We haven't had a racial problem here for fifty years. If the Raintrees aren't white enough, we aren't either. Wonder if the Raintrees were quicker on the up take than we were. Wonder if Miss Emily understood what was starting when we told her about the lawsuit," said Joe.

"Let's ask her and find out what she knows. May be several things going on that we don't know about. May be a lot of people involved, one side or the other," said Jonas.

A visit to the Raintrees confirmed that the new DA, Santini, was up to his eyeballs in it, but they couldn't pin down exactly what it was. Quite a bit of land had changed owners lately - farmland, ranchland. It finally formed a pattern to the North and West of the high valley. Like a twisted sunset, it crouched in the west and waited.

Kate and Ravenwood decided to go ahead with their wedding. Everything was in place, everyone invited. They were going to celebrate. Then they would figure out what Mr. Santini and company were planning.

"They have a lot of nerve, telling the Raintrees they are not American. Is Santini one of those good old American names I've never heard of," asked Kate.

Laughing, Ravenwood fell onto the bed and waited for her to finish her nightly ablutions. He enjoyed watching her in small, daily activities. He enjoyed watching her more every day.

It occurred to him that Santini and his crowd must not be happy with Kate and him. After all, no one was whiter than Kate. Her skin burned easily in the sun. She covered up if she was going to be outside for any amount of time. She considered it a pain, always had. She called it fish-belly white. He called it alabaster and loved the contrast between them. Her skin practically glowed, especially when placed next to his or one of the children. They would get married. Jonas would complete the adoption papers. Then they would figure out what Mr. Santini and friends were up to.

Her wedding day dawned clear and bright. The sun rose in the east just like always, so the world had not done a double back flip and landed on its head. This was good to know. This was a big step for her. Ravenwood was still sleeping beside her. He never slept this late. It was nice – watching him sleep. His face relaxed when he slept. He looked so peaceful. She was sorely tempted to wake him. She wanted morning loving. Just as she was about to speak, Ravenwood rolled her onto her back and began to nibble on her neck. Kate laughed delightedly.

"You were faking," she accused.

"Not really. I just had no reason to move. Then some sexy woman wiggled against me and gave me a reason, a very good reason," said Ravenwood.

"I see," said Kate. "And what do you propose we should do about that."

"I propose we should make morning love and start this day properly," said Ravenwood

"Excellent idea, really excellent," Kate agreed.

Kate had her morning love. Then they showered and she began the pampering, primping, and dressing process. Ravenwood went downstairs. He sent her up breakfast with a small box tucked on the side of the tray – his wedding day gift.

Brynna and Sela flitted in and out of the room, Jonas came to collect Ravenwood's suit. He assured her the children would be properly dressed and ready for the ceremony. The judge would arrive at 1300. Yes, Mr. Po had the food under control. Yes, the cake had arrived. Yes, they had cut the flowers for her bouquet and they were chilling nicely. Yes, he had his tuxedo and his camera and - Jonas finally turned and took her by the shoulders, giving her a small shake.

"Little Mother, everything is under control, everything will be fine. Everything will be beautiful. The gods themselves would never dare to ruin such a day."

"Thank you, Jonas. You are a surprising man," said Kate.

"Just call em like I see em, Kate," said Jonas. "I can't help wishing that you had chosen my bed that first night you arrived. But then, Ravenwood would have damaged me badly, so it's probably best this way."

She remembered thinking Ravenwood had given her a choice of men that first night, but she told herself she was just making it up.

Obviously, she had not been. Did they all know and understand that night? Had they all known? Had they all agreed? Why would they agree? She had just arrived that day, and – STOP THIS! She would make herself crazy. She needed to have a wedding.

"Mama, you look beautiful," said Sela in a whisper.

Kate twirled in front of the mirror, checking herself from all angles.

"One last touch," said Kate, opening the earring box Ravenwood had sent up with her breakfast. She had never seen anything quite like them. She knew they were one of a kind, that no one else had a pair even similar. As she slid them into her ears, Brynna just stood and stared. They completed her wedding dress. They tied everything together. She knew she would wear them constantly. That's why Ravenwood had the extra safety catch put on the back, so she wouldn't be afraid of loosing them. Such strange stones he had chosen. They didn't look like anything she had seen before. There were probably many reasons for his choice. It would be symbolic, well thought out, and completely reasonable. She also knew that the bottom line was – the stones matched her eyes.

On their way down to the side garden, Kate stopped at the kitchen to pick up her flowers. The kitchen was empty, but the smells were scrumptious. Mr. Po had kept the menu a secret and she was tempted to look in some of the pots, but she controlled the urge to peek.

"Sis, you ready to do this?" Joe asked as he appeared in the doorway and stood looking at her with a whimsical expression on his face. "It's been a long time since we had a wedding. Begun to think we'd never have another."

"Yes, Joe. I'm ready," replied Kate calmly.

"Something I wanted to say first. Just take a minute," said Joe.

Kate tensed slightly. She thought she was about to get another confession about that first night and how she could have chosen his bed.

Joe took both her hands in his, saying "Thank you, Kate. I want to make sure you know this. We love you and are so glad you are here, Sis. Ravenwood has always been restless, always wild, and impossible to control really, unless he wants to be controlled. In the past months, I've seen something in his eyes I haven't seen since he was a child, and thought I would never see again."

He paused and Kate just looked at him, waiting.

"Peace, Kate. I've seen peace and it's a wondrous thing. Thank you."

"Thank you, Joe," said Kate.

Joe cocked his head as if to ask why she was thanking him.

"For taking me in, letting me stay, giving me a place to get well," explained Kate.

Laughing softly, Joe said, "Didn't have much choice about that, girl. As soon as the boys described what happened and how you were hurt and they realized where you were, Ravenwood was there like a shot. I knew when I saw him carry you inside that he would do his best to keep you. Gods help us all if you ever decide to leave. There would be no controlling him."

"Not to worry, Joe. You're stuck with me," said Kate.

"Best news I've heard in years, many years," said Joe. "Now, we need to have a wedding here. Where's Big Bill? Where are the children? And where's the groom?" asked Joe in rapid succession.

"Groom is out by the garden. Children are getting restless trying to keep their clothes clean and we need to do this thing before they explode, they're so excited, "said Big Bill.

As they made their way to the garden, Kate recalled any dreams she had experienced about her wedding day. There was no match. Then she recalled any dreams of her ideal man. There was no match. Reaching the garden, she saw Ravenwood and the children waiting for her and she knew this was her dream now. How had it ever been anything else?

The ceremony was brief. The celebration was long. It was mostly family, with a few extras added to the mix. Jonas and Simon Raintree took the pictures. They were good; even the candid shots were good.

"Time we had some music," said Joe. With that announcement, Trist appeared carrying a violin. Kate was thrilled. She had no idea Trist played. She had not heard any practice, but there were many places to practice in the mountains. Then Trist handed the violin to Ravenwood and she was truly mystified.

As he tucked the violin under his chin and made sure it was in tune, she saw sure familiarity and knew he had done this many times for many years. Standing there on the porch, he began to play. Slow and sweet, the music floated across the fields, bouncing against the mountains, filling the sky.

Kate was amazed, as were most people there, who also did not appear to know that Ravenwood played the violin. The music entranced her, as did the movement of his hands, the sway of his body, and the look in his eyes. He was seducing her right there on the porch in front of everyone. Oh, this man was bold. No surprise there, he had been bossing her since the night she arrived. It was his nature to protect, and mostly she just went along. When he crossed the line, she told him about it. She would grab the short stool, the one she stood on to braid his hair, put her hands on her hips and, looking him straight in the eye, she would say, "Give it a rest, Ravenwood," and that would be the end of it.

They would have a lovely night tonight. The more he played, the more she wanted him. He knew that well and he played with it, choosing his music to change her mood, tricky devil! She had not seen this side of him before – and she liked it, she liked it very much.

When Ravenwood finally grew tired, Jamie took his place. The music still was beautiful. It still echoed off the mountains. It still filled the sky, just not quite as much. The differences were subtle. Jamie's music lacked the smoky, sensual flavor that dripped from Ravenwood's playing. It was brighter, with more citrus notes. He was good. Obviously, he had practiced a great deal, but where and when. Moreover, why did he choose to be so secretive about it?

It did not matter. She would ask Ravenwood later. It was a lovely surprise for the reception. She felt him behind her and turned to greet him.

"Thank you Ravenwood. That was lovely," said Kate, turning her face up to his.

"You're very welcome." said Ravenwood, and took a soft kiss for payment. How good she tasted, how good she smelled. He had been right about the earrings. He reached out to touch and set it swaying.

"I've never seen earrings so beautiful, Ravenwood. Thank you," said Kate, hugging him hard.

"Hmgph," was his only verbal reply.

"What are these stones?"

"Those are green diamonds; rare, beautiful, and priceless, just like my woman," said Ravenwood.

A smile lit Kate's face. She literally glowed with happiness. "And most importantly?" she asked.

"They match your eyes. Very difficult, you know. Matching that particular color of green," said Ravenwood.

"Am I rare and exotic, like the diamonds?"

"Oh, yes," said Ravenwood.

"Aren't diamonds the hardest natural substance on earth?

"They absolutely are. They don't break. They survive practically anything short of a nuclear explosion; so beautiful to look at, so thrilling to touch."

"You silver tongued devil," teased Kate. Ravenwood's laughter rang loud and long.

"That is the most amazing thing," said Gully.

"What," asked Jonas?

"The way she can make him laugh," explained Gully.

"Has done ever since the night she arrived," said Joe.

"Emily Raintree regarded the new bride and groom. "They are an unlikely couple in many ways," she observed.

"Hmgph," responded Joe.

"I'm not sure unlikely quite covers it," said Jonas.

"It's no matter. They're good for each other and good for the children. Can't ask more," said Joe with some pride.

The party continued, although the bride and groom soon slipped away for their own celebration.

✣

Several days passed peacefully after the wedding, then something began to bother Kate. She did not immediately know what the problem was, but soon identified it.

Ravenwood, something is wrong. I think its Gabe. Something is very wrong! The phone was ringing as they came in the door.

Kate, we have to go. The ambulance is taking him to the hospital. Luc and Trist are with him, we have to move! So they moved. When they were all at the hospital, Luc and Trist filled them in.: Professor Gilbert had lost his mind and beaten Gabe within an inch of his life. Why and what started it was a mystery. Kate was with Gabe, helping him with The Touch. He reached up and squeezed her hand; this was good, very good.

Ravenwood went over the balcony rail to have a cigar, and run an errand. His visit to Professor Gilbert's house did not take long. They found him in the front yard in the snow, his back cut to ribbons just like Gabe. Then he went back to the hospital; Kate was exhausted and needed his strength now. As he entered the room, he moved up behind her and wrapped his arms around her, allowing his strength to flow into her. Kate breathed easier and so did Gabe. His color was better and the doctor began to believe he would live, miracles did happen. It took hours and thousands of stitches to close his back, but the kid was strong.

No one knew Ravenwood was ever gone, and that was good. When they found his DNA on the balcony post, it was because of the cigar and the trip to smoke it. He had traveled barefoot through town; there were no tracks, and none at Gilbert's house, no trace of his visit.

They had Gilbert in the Emergency Room. Ravenwood would have liked so snuff him, but knew it would be better to let him rot in prison. The prison population had a low tolerance for child abusers. They would punish him every day for the rest of his life, deservedly so. He hoped Gabe lived to appreciate it. He was showing improvement and Kate said he would live. She was never wrong about one of her children.

They stayed at the hospital non-stop, caring for Gabe. It was days before they came home. Everything was fine and they showered and went back to the sickroom. Kate was so worried about Gabe; he was always so frail, but obviously stronger than he looked, thank the gods. He improved every day, little by little. They soon brought him home and Kate took him out in the sun, encouraging him not to cover his scars. Ravenwood also left his uncovered, just to show Gabe not to be a prisoner to his injury. Gabe ran and played like any normal kid and no one made a big deal of the scars on his back. When they found Gilbert, the cops did not enter his apartment, but called an FBI crime scene investigation so there would be no questions about it. The sheriff was, after all, like a son to Ravenwood. They wanted no doubt to linger, no questions unasked. Everything came up clean. One of the police even asked if there were any hawk feathers at Gilbert's place. The local Indians believed Ravenwood could change into a hawk and that is how he traveled without a trace. No one saw him. He left no tracks. It was spooky, having someone around with that kind of talent. It was a good thing they trusted him completely. Of course, things could never be that simple.

The DA, Santini, charged Ravenwood with attempted murder even though he had no proof. The trial would start in 2 weeks. The courtroom was packed. Kate was appalled at them charging Ravenwood when there were so many witnesses to Gilbert's crime. It was clear it was not just a show trial and it would not be quick. Ravenwood's lawyer was Simon Raintree, who was also appalled. There was no excuse for this. As the trial began, Kate looked tired, but beautiful as always. Santini could not resist her and touched her constantly. Finally, Kate had enough.

One day when he grabbed her, she began to scream dramatically and hang onto Ravenwood for protection. (Kate never screamed and never did hysterics or histrionics.) She brought the courtroom to a complete halt and as she stepped back, Ravenwood stepped forward and decked Santini, audibly breaking his jaw. The courtroom was full of police; none made a move to arrest him, they all believed he deserved it. As the ADA made closing arguments, he listed all the things that everyone knew. It was a long list; he thought they were smart.

Simon Raintree had one thing to say. What everyone knew, without any doubt, was if Ravenwood had gone to see Gilbert, Gilbert would be dead. Everyone in the courtroom vocally agreed to that, nodding his or her head for emphasis. The jury never left the room. A voice vote was enough to find Ravenwood not guilty. Ravenwood thanked Simon profusely and Kate gave him a kiss.

Now Ravenwood's trial was over, they would concentrate on Gilberts. Kate was worried that testifying would be hard on Gabe. Kate and Ravenwood both did prep work with Gabe to get ready for the trial. Gabe spoke up clearly and directly. When they asked him to prove what Gilbert did, he peeled off his shirt without hesitation, showing them his scars; the entire courtroom gasped in shock. Gabe behaved as though it was no big deal. Kate was so proud of him! Gabe was proud of himself, rightly so. It was no small thing to survive the way he had. Ravenwood was also proud; Gabe puffed out his chest and strutted. Having his father's respect was very important to Gabe, especially important now.

They convicted Gilbert and sent him to prison. Ravenwood took Gabe to the prison so he could see he was truly safe. It helped a lot, easing Gabe's mind. He knew that Gilbert would not get out of that cage, at least not alive. It pleased him a great deal.

Their lives went back to normal for them, at least what passed for normal most of the time. Gabe took some teasing about his injuries, but Luc and Trist took care of it. It did not last long. People could be so cruel, especially children. Ravenwood just reminded Gabe that what did not kill him made him stronger. He would appreciate it one day, but it was too soon for that.

He did not ask for anything special in the locker room, and did not take any shit from any of them, not really. Just like his mother had suckered Santini into Ravenwood's grasp, Gabe soon demonstrated his power and they left him alone, mostly. There were always one or two saps, but as Kate said, 'It would be so boring without them'. Never underestimate the amusement value. Santini had provided loads all by himself.

Santini went back to the city for what ever he could do there, not being able to talk, and the job of DA returned to Simon Raintree where it belonged. Santini's jaw never did heal properly. It was such a shame, such a handicap for a lawyer. He was no longer a threat to the valley, and the Ravenwoods rejoiced. Many people in the valley rejoiced, not that they wished him pain, they were just glad he no longer threatened their way of life.

Gabe healed well. With his mother's help, the scars faded quickly. Only faint red marks remained to show what Gilbert had done. Gabe was well satisfied that Gilbert was no threat to him now. The visit to the prison clearly demonstrated that for Gabe and he carried no fear. They investigated Gilbert's teaching career and found evidence of many children he abused. Why the children never reported it was a mystery to their parents. None of it was as bad as what he did to Gabe, just casual, random cruelty. It was clear that Gilbert was a sadistic man and he belonged in prison. Ravenwood knew they would carry him out one day, hopefully far, far in the future.

Gabe could not dwell on that day, nor could the rest of the family. It was not worth the angst and they had much better things to do with their time. After all, there were horses to be born and furniture to build, why worry about Gilbert. He was no longer a part of their lives. Thank the gods for that.